MW00440983

The Frannie Shoemaker Campground Series

Bats and Bones

The Blue Coyote

Peete and Repeat

The Lady of the Lake

To Cache a Killer

A Campy Christmas

Also by Karen Musser Nortman

The Time Travel Trailer

Trailer on the Fly

Happy Camper Tips and Recipes

the space invader

A Frannie Shoemaker
Campground Mystery

by Karen Musser Nortman

Cover Design by Aurora Lightbourne

Karen Musser Nortman
2017

Copyright © 2016 by Karen Musser Nortman. All rights reserved. No part of this book may be reproduced in any form by any electronic or mechanical means (including photocopying, recording or information storage and retrieval) without permission in writing from the author.

This is a work of fiction. Names, characters, places and incidents are either the product of the author's imagination, or are used fictitiously, and any resemblance to actual persons, living or dead, business establishments, events, or locales is purely coincidental.

TABLE OF CONTENTS

Chapter One	1
Chapter Two	7
Chapter Three	16
Chapter Four	24
Chapter Five	32
Chapter Six	41
Chapter Seven	51
Chapter Eight	57
Chapter Nine	67
Chapter Ten	75
Chapter Eleven	84
Chapter Twelve	93
Chapter Thirteen	101
Chapter Fourteen	109
Chapter Fifteen	119
Chapter Sixteen	127
Chapter Seventeen	135
Chapter Eighteen	146
Chapter Nineteen	155
Chapter Twenty	160

Chapter Twenty One   170

Happy Camper Tips   181

Acknowledgments   199

About the Author   201

Other Books by the Author   203

CHAPTER ONE

TUESDAY EVENING

BADGER'S BACK THROBBED from the perpendicular metal wall, his butt hurt from the metal bench, and his arms ached from the forced restraint of the handcuffs. He shifted on the uncomfortable seat as much as he could within his limited range of motion. And he still had several more hours to go.

The van lurched to a stop. The glare of gas station lights seeped through the small mesh window separating Badger from his guards.

"I'm first," the driver said. "Those burritos are tearing my insides up." There was a pause, and then, "Mike! Stay awake! I said I'm going to the can!"

Mike groaned. "Yeah, yeah. You try staying awake after getting up at 3:30 in the morning. These double shifts are killing me."

"Tell it to someone who cares. I've done my share. Keep your eyes open 'til I get back. Then you can go get some coffee." The door slammed.

Badger couldn't see the other guard. He leaned forward and rested his elbows on his knees, trying to give his back a little stretch. The floor was littered with small bits of trash—leavings from earlier riders. Gum

1

wrappers, a plastic bag, a bit of wire—he examined the wire, and then the mesh window. Soft snores filtered back—Mike didn't stay awake, as he'd been ordered.

Badger picked up the wire and maneuvered it around toward the lock in his handcuffs, glancing up frequently toward the mesh window. He fiddled with it only a few minutes before he heard the click of freedom. The handcuffs unlocked so easily, that his first thought was that it was a trap. He stared at the window and listened intently. The snores still filtered back.

He wasn't home free—his ankles were shackled and the door was bolted. But the success with the handcuffs spurred him on. What did he have to lose? He was already in for life with no possibility of parole, so they couldn't extend his sentence. The prison shrink had labeled him with a bunch of gibberish that Badger only understood enough to know he was considered hopeless and worthless. That was nothing new. Everyone he'd ever come in contact with had told him the same thing. The old van was headed for a higher security prison than he'd been in the last seven years, and he knew things would only get worse.

He laid the handcuffs on the bench and got on his knees to peer underneath. One support was attached to the bench but not the wall. He grabbed hold and twisted. A grinding screech sounded as the old screw gave way.

Badger jerked his head up and watched the mesh window. Still no sound, other than the snoring. He lumbered to his feet and shuffled to the back. Again, the door jimmied open with the old piece of metal so easily, that he expected a waiting posse outside. But when he eased the door open a crack, empty pavement was brightly lit and stretched over to a row of pines, shrubs, and small trees skirting the edge. The only obstacles were a motorhome and a pickup with a long travel trailer parked at the curb.

He edged the door open further. The other guard could come back from the can at any time. It was now or never. He opened the door far enough to sit on the floor and slide to the ground. At previous stops, the guards hadn't checked on him before pulling out, so he closed the door and fastened it. Maybe they wouldn't check this time either, and it would gain him some extra time.

Crossing the open space was slow because his ankle shackles constricted his steps. He expected a shout from the guard. He went between the back of the trailer and the front of the motorhome, worked through some shrubs, and got down on his hands and knees facing the parking lot so he could peer under the trailer.

It wasn't long until the guard's feet crossed from the convenience store to the prison van. The other guard got out of the passenger side and headed to the restroom.

Badger surveyed his surroundings. The trees and shrubs separated the parking lot from a drainage ditch, which was lined with stones. He scooted toward the ditch and picked up the first rock he saw that looked easy to handle. He sat up, separated his feet as far as the chain connecting his shackles would allow, and used the rock to work on the chain. Traffic noise from the nearby highway masked the pounding, and in minutes the chain broke.

He returned to watching the convenience store lot. The store was one of those with an attached fast food joint—a Subway—and a few people came and went before the second guard returned to the van. Neither man checked the back of the van, and it pulled away from the gas pumps.

Badger let out a breath. These guys worked for a service that the state hired to transport prisoners. It was obvious they just wanted to put in their time and get home—or to the nearest bar.

He weighed his options. He could follow the ditch and possibly get out of town that way. Maybe find some clothes and get the shackles completely off. He probably wouldn't have any luck hitching a ride until he did that.

More people came out of the convenience store, and two sets of feet headed toward the trailer and pickup. Badger edged further into the underbrush. A man opened the driver's door of the pickup.

"Think I'll put my rain gear back in the storage cubby. Doesn't look like I'm going to need it anytime soon around here."

"Good idea," said a woman's voice from the other side of the truck.

The man pulled a rain slicker and pants from the back seat of the truck, wadded them into a bundle, and carried them to a long oblong hatch near the end of the trailer.

He used his keys to unlock the hatch and propped it open while he stowed his bundle.

Badger wished he had a weapon. That truck would be just the ticket out of here. He thought about the rock he had just used with his chain. The guy was old — maybe 50 or 60. Badger was sure he could take him, but the woman would raise an alarm. Besides, he didn't know how to unhook a trailer, and towing it would make him pretty easy to spot by the cops. He could probably figure it out but not fast enough.

The man closed the hatch and climbed into his truck. He started the engine but didn't pull away. Badger figured he must be waiting for the owners of the motorhome.

Badger thought about the hatch in that trailer. There was quite a bit of space in there, and the man didn't lock it — just slammed it shut. It would be a way to get away from the area. He started to get up from his crouch but ducked back down when the driver's door opened again. The man got out. He walked around the front of the truck and yelled, "Hey, Mick! I left my coffee mug in there!"

From his hiding place, Badger saw two other sets of feet coming toward the RVs. They stopped and the man from the pickup walked toward them. They argued in low voices, but Badger focused on that hatch. When all of the feet headed back to the store, he made his move.

He crouch-walked to the trailer, hoping the woman, who was still in the truck, wouldn't glance over and notice him in the side mirror. As quickly and quietly as he could, he opened the hatch and crawled in. The quiet part was hard, what with the chains from his shackles and some poles stored in the hatch, but maybe the general noise around the station would cover it. The hatch was not designed to be closed from the inside for obvious reasons, so Badger fiddled with the latch until it seemed like it might stay closed. Then he lay still, taking a full breath for the first time since he started his escape.

Chapter Two

Tuesday Evening

FRANNIE SHOEMAKER EXAMINED the atlas map of New Mexico with a penlight. Oncoming headlights brightened the cab of the truck briefly, before it returned to the subtle glow of the dash lights.

"How much longer do you think? It looks like about fifty miles to me."

Her husband Larry ran his hand over his crew cut. "Maybe an hour. I hate setting up in the dark—damn that flat tire, anyway."

She reached over and rubbed his neck. "You'd better sleep in tomorrow. It's been a long day."

He grinned. "I think Mickey's planning on hunting aliens first thing tomorrow."

"Let 'im. He can even borrow the truck."

"What if it gets beamed up when the aliens come for him? How would we get home?"

"Easy—take his motorhome. You or Jane Ann can drive it." Frannie's phone chirped for a text message. She picked it up from its niche in the console. "Text from Jane Ann. Mickey says one of our storage doors is flapping."

He winced. "I bet I didn't lock it when I put my rain suit in there." He flipped his turn signal on and slowed, easing over to the shoulder.

Frannie handed him her trailer keys, and he swung down out of the truck. He was back in a minute, returned her keys, and put the truck back in gear.

"Did we lose anything?"

He shook his head. "I didn't look. Too dark."

"I think the battery lantern is in there. That's where I put it the last time I used it."

He shrugged. "Well, it really doesn't matter, because we're not going back for anything."

"Good point."

They continued along in comfortable silence. She had given up on finding a radio station out here in the desert. Roadside signs and house lights were nonexistent. After miles on the straight, usually flat, road, almost deserted by other cars, they were surprised to come over a hill and see a row of taillights stopped ahead of them.

"Huh." Larry leaned forward over the wheel. "What's going on, I wonder? An accident?"

Several patrol cars were parked on both shoulders at the head of the line. Lights flashed over the dark landscape, giving the scattered boulders and scrubby vegetation an otherworldly look.

They eased behind the next car in line. For fifteen minutes, Larry nudged the truck forward every so often as the line moved.

Frannie craned her neck to scan along the shoulder. "I don't see anything up there other than the police."

"I can see that they're searching cars. Probably looking for drugs."

When they finally reached the stopping point, a state policeman walked up to Frannie's window and motioned for her to lower it.

"Yes?" she asked. "What's wrong?"

"Sorry to delay you, ma'am. You're from Iowa?"

"Yes." Frannie had a fleeting thought that maybe they were rounding up all Iowans passing through.

"We have an escaped prisoner — got out of a transport somehow while he was being moved from Santa Fe to Los Cruces. We need to search your vehicles."

"Okay," Frannie said slowly. "Do you want the keys or do you want me to unlock the trailer?"

"Your trailer is locked?"

"Yessir, it has been since we left Texas this morning."

He scratched his head. "Well, you know what? If you've had it locked up, there's no need to search it. We're just worried that this guy has sneaked into someone's vehicle, but looks like he wouldn't have had much chance with you guys. Keep your eyes open and don't pick up any hitchhikers. This guy is a murderer and was already in for life, so he doesn't have anything to lose. Have a good trip, and enjoy New Mexico." He waved them on.

As they pulled away, Frannie grinned at Larry. "Mainly, he thinks we're too old to aid felons."

9

"Maybe, but I'm not complaining. Already this roadblock has cost us another half hour even without a search."

Frannie stared into her side mirror. "I don't think Mickey and Jane Ann were as lucky. She's unlocking the door for another cop. Maybe our friend will go back and convince him to let them go too."

Larry scoffed. "With his mouth, Mickey will be lucky if he doesn't end up in the pokey himself."

"Ohhhh, Mr. Tough Guy. You'd be right there bailing him out if he did."

"Of course I would. How else would I be able to hold it over him for the rest of his life?"

"I should have known." Frannie and Jane Ann, Larry's sister, generally tuned out the ongoing, good-natured arguments between the brothers-in-law. Frannie continued to watch the mirror. "They're coming. Mickey must have kept quiet."

"Or Jane Ann gagged him." Larry chuckled.

A few miles farther on, Frannie pointed out a sign for Deep Pit State Park. "There's our turn."

"None too soon." Larry yawned and turned on his blinker. They turned east and continued another seven or eight miles over rough road to the park entrance.

The landscape had morphed from flat desert to cliffs bordered by strewn piles of boulders. The headlights caught the red stone cliffs looming over one side of the road, as they wound down to the floor of the valley. The truck bounced and jerked as it or the trailer hit one of the

10

numerous potholes. Frannie clung to the overhead handhold to minimize the damage to her internal organs. They had pre-registered and reserved their sites, so they stopped at the guard shack to check in. Larry gave Frannie the campground map, so that she could navigate to their site.

They had spots on the outside ring of the campground, backed up to some scrubby bushes, and behind those, more red sandstone walls. Their set up was pretty minimal and quick because of the late hour. Frannie and Larry unhooked the trailer from the truck, plugged in the electric, and hooked up the water.

"Anything else?" Frannie asked.

Larry shook his head. "I'll get the lawn chairs out of the truck, and we'll leave the rest 'til tomorrow."

Mickey walked over after finishing similar chores with his motorhome. "Too late for a fire?"

"Not only late, but there're no fire rings, and there's a burn ban. There was a sign posted at the check-in. You should be more observant, Ferraro." Larry set up their lawn chairs beside the trailer and pulled a bottle of beer from the cooler.

"I think I'll hit the restrooms before I settle," Frannie said. "Jane Ann? You?"

"Sure." They walked along the road toward a long adobe building with a small tower marking the center entrance. Clear air and a minimum of lights allowed a spectacular display of stars overhead. A small lake to their right glistened.

11

"A more attractive building than most campground restrooms," Jane Ann said.

"I think most of it is a shelter and Visitor Center. But you're right; it is pretty."

They found the restrooms at one end of the building and afterwards tried to look in the windows of the Visitor Center.

"Too dark," Frannie said. "We'll have to check it out tomorrow."

They looked back at the lake and could see a swimming area marked off with ropes and a dock with paddleboats.

"Probably not much swimming in January," Jane Ann said, and they headed back down the road.

Frannie gazed up at the stars and tried to avoid stumbling. "It's been a beautiful trip."

Jane Ann agreed. "It was a rough start — getting snowbound in Missouri, but it was great to spend Christmas with Bob. I wish he could get back to Iowa more often — Mom really misses him — but I know his job makes that difficult."

"And other than the blizzard, the weather's been pretty darn good."

"It has. I'm excited about this part of the trip, too. I'm sure Larry told you, we were here once on a family vacation. But Elaine and I were just toddlers — I don't remember much."

"I know — I'm looking forward to it too."

Back at the campsites, Mickey was describing his plans to go to the UFO Museum in nearby Roswell, which Larry saw as a ripe opportunity for ridicule. "C'mon, Mickey—you don't really believe that stuff."

The women pulled their chairs into the small circle that separated their two campsites.

Mickey was unperturbed. "You can laugh, but you'd be surprised how many groups there are in this area that really believe. Can that many people be wrong? With the size of this universe," his arm swept toward the vast sky, "you don't think there's a possibility of other intelligent life?"

"I hope you aren't including yourself in that 'intelligent life." Larry chortled.

"Nice to see you guys are playing well together," Frannie said.

"While Mickey hangs out with the aliens tomorrow," Jane Ann said, "the rest of us could go to the city museum. There's supposed to be a good collection of bronzes and Native American artifacts there."

"Go ahead. Abandon me. I'll be fine," Mickey said.

Larry grinned. "Don't tempt us."

"I want to see some of the other lakes here, too," Frannie said. "I guess they are old sinkholes that filled in and are really deep."

Jane Ann said to Larry, "We should give Mom a call tomorrow. We haven't talked to her in a week, and she worries if we don't check in."

"I know. She still thinks of us as teenagers."

Jane Ann laughed. "Don't we all? With our own kids, I mean. I heard you give Sally the third degree about her boyfriend the other day on the phone. What is she, 28?"

"Thirty next month," Frannie said. "But still Daddy's little girl."

"Well, I'm turning in," Larry said and got up. "I need my beauty sleep."

Mickey snorted. "You're going to need a lot of it."

"I'll be in soon." Frannie huddled into the blanket she had wrapped around her. "Pretty chilly but the sky is so beautiful."

Frannie and Jane Ann discussed shopping strategies in Roswell and Santa Fe. Jane Ann was planning some purchases for hers and Mickey's first granddaughter and Frannie wanted to look for gifts for her own grandchildren.

Reluctantly, though, she soon had to give in to the demands of her body and give up the good company and starlit night. She said good night and went inside.

As she readied the coffee pot for the morning, she heard a soft clinking sound from somewhere in the trailer. She turned around — it almost seemed like it came from the storage compartment under the couch. One of her ongoing minor concerns was small animals getting into the compartments if they were left open. But that was the one Larry had locked on the road and they hadn't opened it since they arrived.

She shrugged and joined Larry. She hardly remembered getting into bed.

BADGER LAY AS STILL as he could until the truck started up and pulled out on the highway, picking up speed. No way the people in the truck could hear him now. He shifted a little to get off a pipe that was pressing into his back. Then he started to feel around the compartment.

At his feet was the rain gear he had seen the man stash. He ran his hands over a squat heavy object by his elbow, trying to identify it. There was a toggle switch and he pushed it. A harsh white light flooded the compartment. A battery lantern. That could be useful. Overhead zigzag springs held up some kind of cushion. The side of the compartment opposite the hatch was hinged on the bottom—an access door from inside the trailer.

Good to know, but he wasn't interested. He wanted to get out of the trailer, not farther in. This escape had been handed to him, and he wasn't going to screw it up.

The pipe that had poked his back was one of several —two long and one short. He pulled the short one close to him in case he needed a weapon and turned the light off to save the battery. His plan was to sneak out at the next stop and find a phone where he could call his old buddy DeWayne back in Wisconsin.

He needed to get out of this God-forsaken state and the sooner the better. He could use the rain suit to cover his prison jumpsuit and the small pipe as a weapon. The rain gear might be look stupid in this climate but not as bad as running around prison garb.

The ride was bouncy and his hip, elbow, and shoulder soon began to hurt. He had no sense of what direction they were going or how much time was passing, but that was nothing new. He usually didn't know the time in prison either.

He dozed off several times and then jolted awake by a rut or bump in the road. Sometimes the hatch bounced open, and he got a lungful of dust and exhaust. Once he bumped his head and swore loudly, feeling pretty secure in his separate quarters that no one would hear him.

At last he could feel the trailer slowing and hoped it was a gas stop where he could be free of this stuffy box. Then he realized that they had just pulled over on the shoulder, and he could hear the truck still running. He thought about pushing the hatch open far enough to see what was up, but he heard the truck door slam and decided that wouldn't be smart.

Footsteps in the gravel got closer. He gripped the short pipe, as he heard someone fumbling with the latch. But it didn't open; instead he heard the lock click, and the footsteps receded again.

A moment of panic gripped him, as he pictured himself as caged as he had been in the prison van. Then he remembered the hinged inside door. He just needed to be patient. He would get out of here. Maybe these people camped in one of those city campgrounds — that would give him a lot more options. But if not, he would still find his way home. As long as they didn't need anything out of this stupid hole he was in.

Not long after, they slowed again, then made a full stop, moved forward a short distance, and stopped again. This continued, and Badger thought he knew what it was. The cops had set up a roadblock, and they were looking for him. If they opened this compartment, he was screwed. He couldn't go anywhere. Maybe if there was only one cop doing the search, Badger could take him out with the pipe, but then what? He gripped the pipe and waited.

Finally, the trailer started moving again. He took a deep breath, and relaxed his grip on the pipe. He was back to bouncing on the hard floor and sliding into the pipes. The trailer turned and the ride got worse. He had difficulty breathing from the dust that seeped in and the tightness of the quarters. They stopped briefly, and he could hear the driver talking and laughing with another man. Soon they were moving again but not for long. They must be parking because the trailer jockeyed back and forth several times before finally stopping. Next there was some up and down tilting.

He hoped there was nothing they needed out of his hidey-hole. It had to be late. Once they went to bed, he could get out of this dungeon.

He could hear movement and talking all around the outside, and then it quieted again. The trailer bounced as someone came inside, footsteps sounded, and then the floor started to shake and groan. His hiding place started to move slowly sideways as a motor whined and creaked. He figured out that he was in one of those thingamajigs that roll out from the sides of campers. It dropped an inch or so — giving him a clutch of fear — but it stopped, and the motor ground to a halt.

He heard the woman say, "We need to have that slide checked. It's really slow tonight."

"Probably just needs lubricating. I'll check it before we leave here," the man replied. There was more movement in the trailer for about fifteen minutes, and then the door slammed, and the trailer bounced as man and the woman went down the steps.

Badger relaxed a little, but his impatience grew. He wanted to find out where he was so he could plan his next move. Probably out in the country somewhere, judging from the road they came in on.

IT WAS SOME TIME before someone returned inside. Footsteps puttered around and then moved toward the front of the trailer. He could still see a little light around the door that opened into the trailer. One of the people must still be outside.

Finally, the door opened again. He heard more footsteps, some cupboards opening and closing and water running. He wished he had some of that water to get the grit out of his throat. A twitch in his knee caused his chains to clatter. He held his breath until the light around the door dimmed, and the footsteps headed toward the front.

It was quiet. He had to be patient—give them plenty of time to get to sleep. No sound came from outside either. In spite of his discomfort and anticipation of escape, he dozed off.

When he woke, he panicked. Had he slept all night and missed his chance? He had to know.

He gently pushed on the inside hatch near the top and it fell open with a soft thud. A glow from a night-light lit the room, but the windows were dark. Across from where he lay was a kitchen area of sorts—a few cabinets and a small stove. A clock above the cabinets read three-thirty. Good. He still had time.

Badger crawled out, careful to keep his broken shackles from clanking. A doorway toward the front was covered with a curtain. Must be the bedroom. He could hear soft snores.

He pulled the rain gear, the short pipe, and the lantern from the storage area and cautiously closed the door. He saw now that the compartment was under a couch and the access door was actually the front.

The outside door was right across from him. He would have liked to search the cabinets for other useful equipment or get some water but couldn't risk the noise. He tucked the chain ends into the shackles on his ankles and got to his feet. He was stiff and sore from his cramped quarters but put that out of his mind.

In the dim light, the area behind the stove caught his eye. Sticking up from a narrow board along the wall was a row of handles. He pulled one out. It was a short kitchen knife. This was turning out better and better. Clothes of a sort, the lantern, the pipe, and now even a better weapon. He pulled each one up to examine it and selected a mid-sized one.

Clutching his finds, he headed to the door. The latch gave him pause — it wasn't a regular doorknob. He finally got it to release, and remembering how the trailer bounced each time someone used the steps, let himself down ever so slowly until he reached the ground. Not until he had closed the door and heard it latch, did he turn around and check out his surroundings.

There was no moon, but between the stars and a light pole in the distance, he could see trees and shrubs behind the campers. A wall of rock loomed over them. He headed that way.

Once Badger reached the cliff, he found a crevasse to rest in and get his bearings. He hoped none of those damn copperheads were nearby. The local guys in prison talked a lot about snakes and how many they had killed. Probably just bull, but who knew? He pulled on the pants and rain jacket to combat the night chill. The pants were too long, as were the sleeves of the jacket. He rolled them up and put the knife in one of the pockets.

As he gazed over the campground, he saw a light come on in the trailer he had just left. His stomach turned over with a mix of fear and relief. What if he had slept twenty minutes longer? He would have had to get rid of whoever the stupid jerk was that got up so early. That wouldn't have bothered him, but it would have left an obvious trail.

He looked at his feet. Next he needed to get the shackles off and find some decent shoes. The cheap canvas slip-ons they gave them in prison wouldn't do for the journey he had to make, and the iron bands were already chafing his ankles, no farther than he had gone.

His stomach grumbled. And food? Why didn't he take the time to grab something from that trailer? They probably had way more than they needed. His first plan had been to get as far from this place as he could before light, but now he thought he should hang around until he got shoes, food, and water. He would have to watch for someone to leave one of the campers on the edge of the campground, so he could sneak in and get some supplies. How could he be so stupid to think about taking off across the desert without water? But first he would go farther from the campground and get these damn rings off his sore ankles. He could tackle the rest later.

He smiled — a grim grin — as he began to think that this escape was meant to be. The trailer with an unlocked hatch right where and when he needed it. Waking up when he needed to. Clothes. Weapons.

A chaplain in the prison told him nothing good would ever come to him if he didn't change his ways. Well, that wasn't true, was it?

Chapter Four
Wednesday Morning

FRANNIE SAT IN HER lawn chair facing the east. She wore sweat pants, a sweatshirt with the hood up, wool socks, fleece-lined slippers, and was wrapped in a thick blanket. It was 42 degrees, after all. But she knew from looking at the weather back home in Iowa that no way she would be sitting outside *there* watching the sunrise. She'd already been up a couple of hours, finished the book she was reading, drunk several cups of coffee, and dozed in the recliner before moving outside.

The Shoemakers and Ferraros had spent the holidays with Jane Ann and Larry's brother in Texas, visited Mickey and Jane Ann's daughter Justine and her new baby, spent some time in the Texas hill country, and now were headed for Santa Fe. Mickey, a retired English lit teacher, insisted they indulge his closet love of sci-fi with a couple of days in Roswell.

The cliffs rising up on the east side of the campground were part of the escarpment forming a wide barrier of red rock riddled with sinkholes and wandering paths. On the other side, desert stretched into West Texas.

The rosy glow as the sun began its climb emphasized the hue of the cliff, and the beauty of it overwhelmed her. After their long day of driving the day before, made longer by a flat tire on the truck before they even left Texas, she was looking forward to a day of sightseeing and hiking. The online weather site promised a high of 60 degrees, which sounded downright tropical.

The campground was about half full, and people were beginning to stir. Although her back was to the gravel road, she heard footsteps and turned in her chair. A young man, small and fit, with a backpack as big as he was, sweatshirt, hiking shoes and, of all things, shorts, waved and called "Good morning!"

She waved back. "Beautiful day!"

"Sure is." He smiled and turned off the road onto a path leading to the cliffs.

Frannie snuggled more into her blanket and thanked her lucky stars that *she* wasn't out hiking at this hour with that pack. An older man—well, probably the same age as she and Larry—came by with a dachshund on a leash. He'd amble a few steps, stop to let the dog explore interesting scents along the road, walk a few more steps, and repeat.

He looked at Frannie and shrugged.

She laughed. "Kind of hard to get the heart rate up, isn't it?"

He stopped again and smiled. "Actually, this is about my speed."

"I know what you mean. Makes me miss my dog."

He grew serious. "Oh, no. Something happen to it?"

Frannie shook her head. "No, we just had to leave her home with friends. Now I don't have an excuse for a slower pace."

He relaxed and laughed. "I get that." The dog tugged on the leash. "I'm being summoned. Have a nice day." He continued on.

More people emerged from their campers—either wrapped up or shivering. Eventually the door on Ferraro's Class C motorhome, the Red Rocket, opened and Mickey came down the steps, balancing a mug of coffee and his iPad.

"Good morning! Wow, what a view." He looked toward the cliffs.

"Yeah, kind of hard to see much when we got here last night."

He settled in a chair, parked his coffee on the arm tray, and focused on his tablet.

"You're getting as bad as the kids," Frannie said.

"Just wanted to check the news." He scrolled down the screen. "They haven't caught that escapee yet. Says the guards discovered he was missing about fifteen minutes after they left a gas stop in Artesia. That's the town we stopped in. But they got no idea which direction he went. They think maybe he had help."

"I would think it'd be very difficult to find someone out here."

Mickey looked around. "Maybe. On the other hand, there's a lot of open space that it would make it pretty hard to hide."

"Yeah, but then there's places like those cliffs, so if he was traveling just at night, it might not be that tough. I see you made your own coffee this morning." She smiled at him.

"Yeah, thought I'd do it before Larry gets on my case."

"It'll just be something else. You know, if you guys were ever nice to each other, Jane Ann and I would call 911."

Mickey closed the cover on his iPad case. "So we're headed into Roswell this morning?"

"That's the plan." Frannie stretched. "I think we want to do some hiking later when it warms up more."

"Okay, breakfast. How does French toast and sausage sound?"

"As long as you're cooking it and not me."

They both turned at the sound of the trailer door and watched Larry descend the steps, mug in hand.

"I thought you would sleep in after the day you had yesterday," Frannie said. "Were we too noisy?"

"No, you know how it is. When you don't have to get up, you do." He kissed his wife. "You do it every morning."

"True. We were just discussing plans for the day. Go in to Roswell this morning and hike this afternoon?"

"Sounds fine to me." Larry poured himself coffee from the percolator on the utility table. He shook it slightly. "About empty. Mickey, when are you going to start making your own coffee?"

Mickey drew up to his full height, which wasn't much. "I'll have you know, I did this morning. I didn't drink a drop of yours."

"My bad," Frannie said, trying to look contrite. "I've been up a *long* time and drank a *lot* of coffee."

"Lar, did you lose anything yesterday when your hatch was open?" Mickey asked.

"I forgot to check. It was too dark any way. Glad you reminded me." Larry set his mug on the picnic table and pulled his keys out of his pocket. He was only gone a minute or so when they heard him groan and he returned.

"What?" Frannie asked, seeing his face.

"I lost my rain suit. And didn't you say the battery lantern was in there?"

"I think so. Maybe we can report it to the highway patrol and they can keep an eye out for it," Frannie said.

"I've had that rain suit a long time." He carried the coffee pot inside and slammed the door.

"He should have locked it," Mickey said quietly.

"Yes, he only has himself to blame—that's why he's mad. He doesn't like to lose his old stuff."

Mickey heaved himself out of his chair. "Better get to cooking."

"Why don't I cook the sausage? It'll be faster, and you won't have to do all the work."

He gave her his impish grin. "Suit yourself. I'll bring it out. I'm going to cook the French toast outside."

"I'll do that too and not smell up the trailer."

AFTER FILLING THEMSELVES with sausage, French toast, and eggs, they piled in Larry's truck for the trip to Roswell. They dropped Mickey at the UFO museum, and told him they would pick him up in an hour and a half, if he was still a resident of earth.

The Shoemakers and Jane Ann spent a pleasant time at the city museum admiring the art collection, Native American and pioneer artifacts, and Robert Goddard's relocated workshop. Jane Ann and Frannie browsed the gift shop and purchased some turquoise earrings for Larry and Jane Ann's mother and some unusual rocks for Frannie's grandson Joe. They walked out into the sun, discussing the display of beadwork and Rogers Aston's bronzes. Larry had been waiting by a fountain for the women.

"Mickey would have really enjoyed this place if he wasn't so stubborn," Jane Ann said.

"And he'll never admit that the UFO one is hokey," Larry said.

He didn't. He was waiting outside for them. When he climbed back in the truck, Larry said, "So they rejected you."

"You know, Shoemaker, those of us with imaginations just have to be patient with the rest of the world until you see the light."

Jane Ann eyed the sack that he stuffed down in the foot well. "What did you buy?"

Mickey beamed. "Just a little UFO. A simple drone — remote control, spinning lights — "

"Oh, Mickey, you don't need more toys..." Jane Ann said. "How much was it?"

Mickey sputtered. "It's for our granddaughter!"

Jane Ann laughed. "Teresa hasn't even been born yet."

Larry grinned. "Joe would like it."

"Buy for your own grandkids. Well, maybe he and I can try it out until Teresa's old enough. I'm not even going to get it out of the box now. So there. How about lunch at that Italian place that we saw in the tour guide?"

"That's where I'm headed," Larry said.

AFTER LUNCH, THEY stopped at a local winery, where Mickey was excited to purchase some Alien beer. They discovered the proprietor had gone to college with one of Larry and Jane Ann's cousins and another customer had lived in Iowa before retiring in New Mexico. Old home week.

Before they returned to the truck, they walked along the main street, enjoying the motifs of aliens and spaceships on many of the stores, from coffee shops to gift shops.

A stop at a grocery store snagged some chorizo, sweet potatoes, and rice for a casserole Jane Ann planned to concoct for supper. Frannie picked up a loaf of locally made seven-grain bread. Before he pulled out of the parking lot, Larry ran back in to the store for a half-gallon of tin roof sundae ice cream.

"A nice day," Jane Ann said, as they headed back to the campground. "I loved that museum."

Mickey nodded. "Don't forget my drone—*and* Alien beer."

Larry craned his neck as he pulled the truck out into the street. "I'm sure you won't let us forget it, Mick."

"It was a nice day. But I do think the hiking to the lakes can wait until tomorrow," Frannie said. "I'm ready for a nap."

HER NAP WAS DELAYED. When they returned to the campground, a sheriff's car was parked by their campsites.

CHAPTER FIVE

WednesdayMorning

BADGER WAS COLD, especially his feet. After resting in the crevasse for a short while, he began to consider what might be living in the cracks and started hiking up a path that wound between rows of rocks. It was still dark and he stubbed his toe a couple of times. The chains clanked as he walked. Once he reached the top of the hill and descended a little on the other side, he turned the lantern on, found that he could switch it to low, and looked for a suitable rock to use as a hammer. There were lots of choices. Selecting one, he found a seat and began to work on the right shackle. Any way he pounded on it resulted in glancing blows on his anklebone and foot. He gritted his teeth. After thinking that everything was going his way, he realized he had screwed up on several counts.

His plan had been to get the shackles off, and then get as far away from this place as he could before full light. That was before he realized that striking off across the desert without food or water would be pretty stupid. He decided he needed to watch the campground for people to leave their campers and break in for some water and food. There were water hydrants in some places, but he had nothing to carry it in.

The right shackle finally broke, but he could feel blood trickling down his ankle. He started on the left one. The sky was beginning to lighten. That helped his mood a little.

He tried to put his mind to how the cops might be thinking. He had been assuming that they would expect him to head to Mexico. Maybe that was wrong. Maybe they would be looking for him to go back home. But he had no family there—well, not that he knew of. He'd spent his whole childhood in foster homes and the juvie system. And he'd never been married—couldn't find a girl worth settling down for. He hadn't talked to Dewayne in a couple of years. Maybe Dewayne didn't even live there any more.

He could decide later. The first order of business was to get supplies. The left shackle split, accompanied by excruciating pain as the rock scraped his anklebone. He stuck the shackles behind a nearby rock not visible from the path and put his so-called shoes back on.

Starting back along the path toward the campground side of the escarpment, he heard noises up ahead. He ducked behind a large boulder. Coming up the path was a young man, about Badger's size. He bent under a large backpack, watching his footing as he climbed.

Badgered grinned to himself. Another lucky break. He fingered the knife in his pocket but then thought about the short pipe. Less suspicious — it might look like an accident. He hefted the pipe, waited until the footsteps neared his hiding place, and stepped out on the path.

The young man looked up and began to smile. "Oh, hi..."

Badger swung the pipe and caught the guy just above the ear, producing a satisfying crunch. The hiker went down, with kind of an 'oof' sound, and didn't move. Badger went to work pulling off the backpack and the guy's sweatshirt. He took off the rain jacket and was going to throw it over the cliff, but stopped.

This guy had hair similar to his own and was about the same size. So he put the rain jacket on the hiker — no easy task. The guy was dead weight. Badger chuckled. He was such a funny guy — Dewayne always told him so.

Then he untied the guy's hiking shoes and pulled those off, along with the heavy socks. He slipped his prison shoes on the hiker's skinny feet and said, "*You* don't have to worry about *your* feet getting cold any more."

The hiker's socks felt great, and although the shoes rubbed his sore ankles, he knew he would be better off in the long run. Maybe the guy had some Band-Aids or something in his backpack, but right now, Badger needed to get out of sight. He dragged the hiker over to the cliff edge and pushed him over. The body didn't fall far, but it was enough to explain the injury to his head. Badger headed east.

BY THE TIME the sun was fully up, he had reached the edge of the rocks and looked out over unending desert. Time to take a break. The backpack weighed a ton. Maybe he could discard some of it and lighten up a bit. Inside, he found a couple of bottles of water, some canned stew and vegetables—who takes vegetables on a hike? The guy had probably been some kind of vegetarian tree-hugger or something. 'Course the stew had meat, so maybe he wasn't. Who cares?

He opened one of the bottles of water, downed the whole thing, and tossed the bottle over his shoulder.

Next he picked up a can of stew and examined it. It didn't have one of those pop-off lids. He rummaged in the backpack but couldn't find a can opener. So how the hell was the guy going to eat it? It occurred to him then that guy probably had some kind of opener in his pocket. Should he go back for it? By now, other people would be out hiking, and he could run in to someone. His other option was to get into a camper and find an opener. But taking one off the body would sure be easier.

He stashed the backpack and covered it with stones. It was frustrating to backtrack, but had to be done. When he got to the spot where he had pushed the hiker over, he stopped and listened carefully. Sure enough, he could hear voices coming up the path—

including at least a couple of loud brats. He ducked behind an outcropping and flattened himself against the rough wall.

"Mom!" yelled a little girl. "Can we climb those rocks?"

"No!" The answer was firm. "We have to stay on the path."

"You're too little, any way," an older boy said in a singsong voice.

Badger edged back around the wall to stay out of their sight.

"Shut up, Justin. You're not the boss of me."

"Carrie, don't talk that way," a man said. "Justin, get down off those rocks."

"Aw, gee..." Footsteps slapped the ground running on up the path.

Badger worked his way completely around the rock column and took a quick look up the path. The family was just disappearing.

He returned to the cliff edge and looked over. If he was careful, he could get down to the body. If someone else came along, he could say he was trying to help the fallen hiker. Then he could send them for help and skedaddle. That would work.

He let himself down carefully, searching for each foothold. Once he got close, he could reach one pocket. It was weird, searching a dead guy's pocket, and it was useless—there was nothing there. He would have to turn the body over to get to the other side and back pockets, because there wasn't any perch that would allow him to reach far enough otherwise. He grabbed a leg and tugged the body slowly toward himself. As he reached toward the pocket, stones below the body began to roll and tumble down, and Badger felt the weight of the body pull away from him. He either had to let go or end up at the bottom himself.

He watched the body slide another twenty feet. If the guy had a can opener, he could keep it. Badger worked his way back up to the path. When he reached the edge, he grabbed a tree root and rested his head a minute on his arms.

"What's goin' on?" said a gravelly voice above him.

Badger looked up into the face of an old lady with flyaway white hair. She was dressed for hiking, and her face was as weathered as an old nut.

He pointed down at the barely visible body. "A guy must have...fallen...I tried to get...to him, but..." He didn't have to fake being out of breath. "Can you get help?"

The woman leaned over. "Better help you up first, son, or you'll end up down there with him." She bent over grabbed Badger's forearms with a surprisingly strong grip, and Badger managed to get footholds to get back on the path. He bent over, hands on knees, panting.

She grabbed his arm. "You come down with me. Someone oughta look you over. What you did to try and help that guy — you're kind of a hero, you know."

Was he going to have to send this dame down to join the hiker?

"No, I'm fine. I just need to catch my breath. Can you go get a ranger or someone to help?"

She looked doubtful, but said, "You sit down and wait, okay?" She guided him to a flat rock. He sat.

"I'll be fine," he repeated. "Do you want me to go for help and you stay here?" He sure as hell hoped she said no.

"Oh, no, you need to rest. I'll be right back." She hurried back down the trail toward the campground. She glanced back over her shoulder several times until she disappeared around a bend in the path.

As soon as she was gone, Badger jumped up and took off in the opposite direction. He decided not to go back to where he stashed the backpack. Instead he would take one of the offshoots of the trail in case they tried to follow him. He soon came to another branch and took it. After several more turns, he spotted what looked like a small cave up above the trail. If he could hide up there, he could keep an eye out for anyone who might be looking for him.

The rounded rocks made for precarious foot and handholds. Once he started to slip and caught himself but ripped one knee of the rain pants. Behind him the sun rose higher, bringing a little but much welcomed, warmth. Finally he was able to crawl in to the cave and pull back enough that he couldn't be seen unless they climbed up to his level.

But the cave made him nervous. He hated snakes ,and this looked like a good place for them. He moved back out in the front of the cave and scanned what he could see of the path. It would take them a while to haul the hiker up and even then, they wouldn't be able to tell that he hadn't just fallen over the edge of the cliff, so maybe they wouldn't come looking for him until later in the day. He didn't know how long one of those autopsy things took. Maybe he was just wasting precious time here. He couldn't decide what to do.

He watched the sun measure the minutes and hours. It must be at least an hour or two since the old lady had gone for help. Okay, he'd been doing nothing long enough. It would be better if he was on the move, anyway, than a sitting duck up here. He climbed down and continued on the path, taking a couple more turns. Judging from the sun, he was sure he was still going toward the desert side, not the campground side. But when he had walked an hour or so and turned around in a couple of dead ends, he became disoriented. The sun was now overhead, so that didn't help much.

He sat down on a rock and scratched his head. All around him were red rock walls, and the path seemed to be narrowing — almost closing in on him. After his years in cells, this kind of confinement made him batty. He tried to remember which way he had turned the last couple of times but no luck. He was thirsty and needed water — water that he had left in the backpack. He pulled up the sleeves of the sweatshirt and loosened the string in the hood.

Badger heard a buzzing sound behind him. It startled him because it had been so quiet. He jerked around, lost his balance, and threw out his arm to catch himself. A sharp pain pierced his hand at the same time that he felt a cold scaly surface—not rock. He jumped up and turned around to see a small snake, covered with brown spots, slither down to the path.

Badger screamed in rage, pain, and frustration. He lashed out with his foot, fortunately protected by the hiking shoe, and stomped the snake. It stopped, writhed a little, and lay still.

He felt panic engulf him. He'd heard the noise the snake made—it must be some kind of rattler. The bite was on the outside of his left hand. It was not very large but it hurt.

He tried to remember how they treated snakebite in the movies. Maybe a tourniquet? Some tough guys in old Westerns sucked out the venom and spit it out. He couldn't see himself doing that. Without even looking up at the white sun, he barreled headlong down the path.

CHAPTER SIX

WEDNESDAY AFTERNOON

SINCE THE SHERIFF'S CAR was blocking his parking spot, Larry pulled his truck into a neighboring empty site. They piled out with their sacks and packages and walked toward their campers. The sheriff was leaning against his car, and Larry stopped to introduce himself. Frannie followed and stood behind him.

The sheriff was a large trim man with a mustache who reminded Frannie of the old Dennis Weaver TV character, McCloud. He offered Larry his hand. "Shoemaker, you say? Is this your trailer?"

"Yes it is."

"Mr. Shoemaker, do you recognize this?" The sheriff leaned in the open window of his cruiser and pulled out a large, clear plastic bag and held it up.

Larry's eyes opened wide. "It looks like my rain suit—or part of it anyway. Did someone turn it in? How did you find us?"

The sheriff shifted and squinted his eyes. "Did you lose it?"

Larry explained about having the hatch door on the trailer come open and losing the rain suit, plus the battery lantern. "I certainly didn't expect an officer to take the time to return it. Thank you." Larry reached for the bag, but the sheriff drew it away, like a child playing 'keepaway.'

"This wasn't found in a ditch, Mr. Shoemaker."

Larry stopped reaching and looked at him more closely. "What do you mean? Where did you find it?"

The sheriff paused for effect. "We *found* it on the body of a man who apparently fell off a cliff." He jerked his head toward the cliffs behind them. "We think he's the escaped convict we've been looking for. We *think* he had help." He waited.

"Oh!" Frannie said. "They told us about that when they stopped us in the roadblock yesterday."

"Yeah?" the sheriff said, turning to her. "Did they search your vehicles?"

Frannie began to see where this was going. "Nooo..."

"They saw we were from out of state and when we told the officer that our trailer had been locked since we left Texas that morning, he decided it wasn't necessary," Larry said. "What are you implying?"

"I'm just trying to find out what happened. How this guy got here, and where he got a change of clothes and a raincoat," the sheriff said. "Your name was in the neck of the raincoat." Despite the sheriff's disclaimer, accusation hung in the air.

"Sheriff," Frannie said, "My husband is a retired police officer. There's no way he would help an escapee."

"I didn't say he did," the sheriff said, "but I'd sure like to know how the guy got this coat."

"So would I," Larry said.

"We're from Iowa," Mickey jumped in. "We never even heard the guy's name, but I'm sure we don't know him. He obviously found the coat along the highway."

"Baxter Bagley, better known as Badger. And he's from Wisconsin. That's pretty close to Iowa. And I doubt very much that he walked along the highway if he was trying to escape."

"Good Lord!" Mickey said. "His mother must have hated him to saddle him with a name like that. What a handle for a crook!"

"Murderer—" the sheriff started to say, but a deputy came up and touched him on the elbow. The sheriff turned, and the deputy handed him an ID.

"This was in a hidden pocket in the shorts," the deputy said.

The sheriff moved away and the deputy followed. They conferred; the sheriff rubbed his jaw, looked back at the group, and gave the deputy instructions. As the deputy left, the sheriff called after him, "Ask Ranger Hill if there is or has been anyone registered here by that name."

When he returned, Larry said, "So the dead man isn't the escapee?"

The sheriff drew up to his full height. "Maybe, maybe not. He could have stolen those shorts."

"What made you think it was the convict in the first place?" Mickey asked.

"General description, prison shoes," the sheriff said almost absently, as he watched the deputy head toward the Visitor's Center. Then he caught himself and turned back. "You're not off the hook. Somebody helped that guy. I'll be back to talk to you later." He got in his car, waited for them to move away, and drove off.

"WELL! I THINK I need a beer and I'm not even the one they suspect. Shoemaker? My treat and I'll fix some nachos," Mickey said. They followed him over to the lawn chairs by Mickey and Jane Ann's coach.

Once they were seated, Jane Ann said, "How *would* the guy have gotten your coat, Larry? The sheriff is right—if you were trying to escape the authorities, you wouldn't walk along the highway."

Larry shrugged. "They aren't sure the man in the rain coat is the escapee. More likely someone who was hitchhiking along that road."

Mickey came out of their camper with a tray of nachos and set it on the table. "Except most hitchhikers don't wear prison shoes. Bad for the feet."

"Mickey, when you found the story this morning about the escape, did they have a photo of him?" Frannie asked.

"Sure. Why?"

"Go get your tablet. I want to see it."

Mickey huffed but got up. "You could get your laptop."

She smiled sweetly at him. "But I'm all comfortable, and yours is closer."

When her returned, he had found the story and handed Frannie the tablet. "Doesn't he remind you of Larry?"

Frannie laughed. "Hardly." The photo, which could have been either a mug shot or from a driver's license, showed a sullen, craggy face, brown short hair, a scruffy beard and unfocused eyes. "Don't think I've ever seen him. Although I dated a guy once..." She grinned and passed the tablet to Larry and Jane Ann. They both shook their heads and gave the tablet back to Mickey.

Mickey got serious. "Larry, you didn't check that cubby until this morning. Was it unlocked last night?"

Larry shook his head. "Remember, I locked it on the road and didn't open it last night because I didn't need anything out of it. Why?"

"Just thought maybe someone could have gotten the rain suit and lantern out of it then. You'd think if it had fallen out on the road, we would have noticed it. We were almost always right behind you."

Frannie shuddered at the thought of someone getting something out of their compartments while they were sleeping.

"Yeah, but it was dark," Larry said.

"Are you sure nothing else is missing?" Jane Ann asked.

"Not really." Larry glanced over at his trailer. "Do you have all your compartments memorized?"

Mickey laughed. "'Course not. Some of that stuff has been in there since the dawn of time."

"You've only had that coach four years," Larry said.

"Okay, since then. So what else do you keep in there?"

"The grill and poles. Some rope lights. I think Frannie has some plant hangers in there."

They all sat wrapped up in their own thoughts.

Finally Larry sighed and got up. "Now you've got me curious," he said to Mickey. "Happy?"

"Yup."

He returned with a scowl on his face.

"What's the matter?" Frannie asked.

"The cross piece for the grill stand is gone, too. That short pipe that the chain goes through? I always put those pipes clear to the back."

"That's really odd. I still think we would have noticed that much stuff falling out on the road," Mickey said.

"Was that hatch flapping open very often?" Frannie asked.

"We texted you as soon as we noticed it," Mickey said.

Larry scratched his head. "I don't think we've had our grill or lantern out in a week or more—we used yours in Fredericksburg—but I definitely just put the rain suit in there when we were stopped in Artesia. We were waiting for you, and I noticed it in the back seat. I figured

I wasn't likely to need it in New Mexico, so put it back there."

Mickey rubbed his chin and looked up at the sky. "Aliens probably could have gotten in there."

"That's really helpful, Mick."

"Good afternoon." It was the man with the dachshund that Frannie had seen earlier. "Do y'all know what's going on? I saw you talking to the sheriff."

"Someone fell off one of the paths up there." Larry pointed up at the cliffs behind them. He didn't elaborate on the sheriff's suspicions.

"Really? We've been gone most of the day."

"Us too," Larry said. "I'm Larry Shoemaker, by the way."

The man held out his hand. "Palmer Pierce. I see you're from Iowa?" He nodded toward the truck license plate. He was tall and straight, with a mane of silvery-white hair that emphasized his heavy tan.

"Yeah, we're headed up to Santa Fe and then back towards home. You?" Mickey said. He opened up another lawn chair and offered it to Palmer.

"Been in Arizona and thought we might stay there longer, but we like to be on the move, so we decided we would take our time and go home along the Gulf."

"Where's home?" Frannie asked.

"Maryland. Baltimore. So someone fell, you say? Were they hurt or—" The words hung in the dry air, expecting an ominous response.

Larry nodded, and his voice was grim. "He was dead."

"Do they know who it was?" Palmer Pierce asked.

"Not for sure."

"Reason I'm asking is there's a young guy camping in a tent next to us who left on a hike early this morning, and we haven't seen any sign of him since we got back. My wife told him we were going to a winery today and he asked us to bring him back a bottle—gave her money to do it."

"I think I saw him this morning, right before you came by!" Frannie said.

Palmer nodded. "That's him. He left right before I took Schneider for her walk. Sure hope nothing's happened to him."

Frannie sat stunned. It hadn't occurred to her that the body they found could be someone she had seen that very morning.

"Maybe you should report it to the ranger," Larry said.

"I will," Palmer said. He got up and untangled Schneider's leash from his chair. "Well, I 'd better be getting back or I'll miss supper." He patted his barely noticeable belly. "As you can tell, that doesn't happen often."

Right, thought Frannie. But they all smiled and waved, as he tugged the dachshund back out to the road.

"Speaking of which, we need to get ours going," Jane Ann said to Mickey. "Do we have charcoal so we can use that grill?" She pointed at the permanent grill near the picnic table.

"We do," Larry said.

"I hope it wasn't in that back cubby," Mickey said.

"No, it's in the truck. I'll get it." They busied themselves with fire building, browning, stirring, and table setting. As Frannie spread the tablecloth, she saw ranger's truck stopped by a big fifth-wheel next to a tent across the campground.

Jane Ann prepared a fragrant stew in her Dutch oven on the grill. While she was spooning it into a big bowl, Frannie went in to slice the bread. As she pulled the bread knife out of the rack, she noticed the slot next to it was empty. Larry. When he dried the dishes, he always forgot about the knife rack and threw all of the knives in one of the drawers. Hard telling where she'd find it.

It was a simple supper, but they savored the combination of spicy sausage, tomato sauce, and sweet potatoes, mellowed by garbanzo beans and crunchy wild rice. Mickey opened a bottle of Cabernet and they discussed the day and the escaped convict. They were just finishing their meal when the ranger pulled up.

"Evening, folks," he said, as he got out of his truck.

"Beautiful campground you have here," Mickey answered, by way of greeting.

"Thank you. But disturbing events here today." The ranger took a toothpick out his mouth and stuck it in the pocket of his shirt. "Mr. Pierce over there says one of you saw Mark Cullen go by this morning."

Frannie spoke up. "I don't know his name, but a young man in hiking clothes went by—maybe about 7:00? Kind of a small man, short dark hair, scruffy beard."

The ranger nodded. "Mark Cullen. He was the victim they found this morning up on the rocks."

"But—" Frannie stopped, puzzled and sad. "The sheriff said he was wearing my husband's rain coat and prison shoes. The guy who went by here had hiking books and a Kansas Jayhawks hooded sweatshirt on."

"Which makes it look like it wasn't an accident," Larry said.

The ranger didn't comment on that. Instead, he said to Frannie, "Did you see which way he went?"

Frannie pointed out the trail the hiker had taken.

"And he was alone?" the ranger asked.

"Yes, definitely."

"Okay. So apparently, the escaped felon is still on the loose, and it seems more than a coincidence that we had a violent crime here. I want to caution you folks not to be out alone and stay alert." He made this warning in an automatic tone that suggested he wasn't sure they were entirely in the dark about Badger Bagley's whereabouts, but it was his duty to caution them anyway.

He was headed back to his truck when three teenaged boys ran out of the path to the cliffs, yelling.

"Help! Ranger! Help!"

CHAPTER SEVEN
EARLIER WEDNESDAY AFTERNOON

BADGER STUMBLED ALONG the path blindly, clutching his left hand. He remembered a first aid kit in the hiker's backpack, but he had no idea how to get back to where he had stashed it. Although it wasn't very hot, the rock walls protected him from any wind, so the sun warmed him and made him thirsty. He also felt like he had a fever.

He came to another turn and paused. Voices and scraping noises were coming from the right. Must be the cops. He knew if he could get back to where they were, he could find the path to the backpack, but of course that wouldn't be smart until the cops were gone. He took the path to the left. His mind was on the snakebite, and he randomly turned at each junction of the path without thought.

The path jogged and, as he rounded a rocky outcropping, he saw someone up ahead. The old lady with the flyaway hair. He started to back up, but she turned around, and her face lit up.

"There you are! I was so worried! I'm afraid you must have hit your head." She used her walking stick to climb the slight slope back toward him.

He just stood there. He couldn't think. His hand was swollen and painful and he was dizzy. If he tried to get away, he wasn't sure he could even outrun her.

She set her small backpack down and reached in. He pulled back into the rocks—what if she had a gun? She pulled out a bottle of water and held it out to him.

"You must be thirsty. Here." Suddenly she didn't look so threatening and reminded him of a grandmother he used to imagine having. He took the bottle, but his left hand was shaking, and he couldn't open it. She reached for it back, but he hung on to it. This was confusing. What did she want?

She gently pulled the bottle away, opened it, and handed it back to him, watching his face the whole time.

He guzzled the water and started to pitch the bottle, but she took it away from him again and put it in her pack. He could see where this was going. She wanted his fingerprints. He would have to take care of her too, but first maybe she could help him.

"I'm lost," he said. "I can't find my way back." He rubbed his throbbing hand.

"Back where? Did you come from the campground? What's the matter with your hand?"

Too many questions. "Nuthin'. Just a little bite. I was trying to get to the side away from the campground."

She shook her head. "You don't want to go that way. There's nothing for miles except for desert. I think you're confused. What's your name?"

"Jim," he said. Good thinking. She may have seen about his escape on the news. "What's yours?"

She smiled, wrinkling her brown face further. "Elizabeth Anne Mary Victoria Pryce."

"Wow. That's quite a handle."

"You can call me Liz. My father was English and named me for all of the queens of England."

That didn't make sense to him, but whatever. "Well, I gotta be goin'. Which way to the desert?"

"Please think about that. Do you just want to see it? Actually, the ranger would like to talk to you and thank you for trying to help that young man. I wish you had waited there. That's why I came to find you." She laid her gnarled old hand on his left forearm and he winced. "What's wrong?"

He jerked his arm away. "I told you—I got a little bite."

She cocked her head. "What kind of bite?"

"Rattlesnake, I think."

"Let me see it."

He hesitated and then held out his hand, palm down.

Liz examined it and looked up into his face. "It definitely looks like a snakebite. Did you see the snake?"

"Yeah, and it made a noise right before it bit me—a buzzing sound."

"How big was it?"

He held his hands up about two feet apart. "It had brown spots."

She let go of his hand and stuck her hands in the back pockets of her jeans. "You may be lucky. It sounds like a desert massasauga. Their venom is pretty potent, but they're too small to deliver much of it."

"Are you a teacher or something?"

"No, I'm a retired archeologist. But you need to get medical attention."

"No!" He pulled his hand back as if she was going to grab it again. "I mean, I can't."

"What do you mean, you can't?"

"I—I don't have any money—or insurance."

Liz put her hands on her hips. "They will still treat you."

"I don't have time—I have to get home. My grandma's very sick."

"Where does she live?"

"Uh—Oklahoma."

"Where in Oklahoma? Oklahoma City? Tulsa?"

"Yeah, Tulsa."

"So how are you going to get there? Do you have a car?"

"Uh, it's at the other end of the park." He pointed in what he thought was a northerly direction.

"So let me give you a ride there. You'll be able to get to Tulsa that much quicker."

He thought about it. It was one way to get out of this place. But almost too late, he remembered the cops who would be crawling all over the place. He pulled back and shook his head.

She picked up her backpack and reached for her walking stick. "What are you afraid of? C'mon—let me help you back to the campground and I can drive you to a clinic..."

Badger turned and rushed off in the opposite direction. He wanted to knock the old woman down and take her supplies, but couldn't quite bring himself to do it. After he had ducked down several side paths, he stopped and caught his breath. He was an idiot. He *should* have taken the old lady's bag. What was she going to do, anyway? Even if she screamed, nobody would probably hear her.

As that thought crossed his mind, he heard somebody yelling. A high, thin voice calling "Jim! Jim! Where are you?"

At first Badger thought someone else must be wandering around these rocks, but then he remembered telling the old lady that that was his name. Here was his chance to get that bag—then he wouldn't have to worry about finding the other backpack. He waited until the calls came closer and stepped out into the path.

"I'm sorry," he said, with difficulty—he wasn't experienced in apology—"I need to see my sick grandma, and I can't take time to go back."

She walked closer, no sign of fear on her face. "Jim, you will be able to make much better time if you are feeling well. That snakebite isn't likely to kill you, but your hand could be come infected, you may get fever —"

She stood in front of him now, the pack peeking enticingly over her shoulder.

"I'll be fine," he insisted.

She leaned her walking stick against the rocks in order to shrug her backpack off. Badger grabbed the stick and swung it along side her head. She crumpled to the ground without a sound. He dropped the stick, and as he bent over to finish pulling the bag off her shoulders, said, "I guess you never heard, lady, that nice guys finish last."

He slung one strap of the pack over his shoulder and scurried off along the trail.

CHAPTER EIGHT

WEDNESDAY EVENING

THE THREE BOYS SKIDDED to a stop in front of the ranger, tumbling in to each other, and all tried to talk at once. The ranger said, "One at a time." He pointed to the tallest and said, "You. What's going on?"

"There's a lady on one of the paths — "

"She's hurt or maybe dead," interrupted another, a redhead.

The third pointed to his head, above his ear. "She's bleeding here."

"Okay." The ranger pulled out a walkie-talkie. "I'll need one of you to lead me back there. Can you find the spot again?"

They all nodded vigorously.

"Is she alone?"

The tall kid shook his head. "Our friends, Kyra and Bailey, stayed with her."

"Good," the ranger said. He turned aside to give instructions over the radio. He pointed to the tall boy and the redhead. "You guys wait here and show the EMTs where to go." To the third boy, he said, "You show me where she is."

The other two boys looked around, at a loss for what to do now that they had delivered their news.

Frannie called over to them, "Boys, would you like some water or a soda while you wait?"

They both looked relieved and walked over. One asked for water and the other a Mountain Dew, but settled for Pepsi. Larry offered them seats at the picnic table where they could watch the road—just in case sirens weren't enough to herald the emergency vehicles. They sat, fidgeting and jerking their heads around at every noise. Their faces were pale in spite of their summer tans.

After introductions were made—the tall boy was Gus and the redhead went by Spider—Frannie asked, "Kind of late to be hiking in those hills, isn't it? Weren't you afraid of getting lost?"

"We *were* lost," Spider said, his eyes wide. "We had *just* figured out where we were when we *found* that lady."

Gus agreed. "Lucky we did, or we might not have made it back here in time for help."

"So you think she might still be alive?" Jane Ann asked.

Gus's face sagged. "Dunno. I hope so."

"I've got some chips and salsa," Mickey said. "Would you like some?"

"Sure," Spider said. "We didn't get any supper yet."

Frannie smiled at the forthright honesty of youth—and noticed that Gus kicked his friend under the table.

"I mean," Spider hurried to add, "if it's not too much trouble."

"Not at all," Mickey said and went in his camper.

"We could also fix you some sandwiches," Jane Ann said.

Gus shook his head. "We'll be fine. Is it all right if we leave our packs here?"

"Of course," Frannie said.

Mickey came back out with the snacks and set them in front of the boys.

"Did you know the woman who was...hurt?" Frannie asked.

Spider shook his head, his mouth full of chips. "Kyra does. I think the lady lives in Roswell."

Gus watched the road intently and, as soon as flashing lights became visible in the gathering dusk, jumped up from the bench. Spider followed him, and they called out their thanks as they headed to the road. The rescue unit pulled over at the hiking path, and the EMTs were met by the two boys.

THE SHOEMAKERS AND FERRAROS continued sitting around their campsite for the next hour. Darkness enfolded the area, and Frannie missed having a campfire. Besides it was chilly. They discussed possible summer camping trips, gossip that Mickey had picked up from a phone call home, Larry and Mickey's expectations on the golf course in the spring, and every other inconsequential subject they could think of to keep their minds off what was happening in the hills.

"We're planning on leaving tomorrow and heading to Santa Fe, right? That is, if the sheriff lets us leave," Larry said.

"Yeah," Mickey said. "But don't let me forget to gas up in Roswell. I should have gotten gas when we stopped at Artesia—don't know why I didn't."

"You were concentrating on stocking up on Snickers," Larry said with a grin.

"Well, as beautiful as this place is, I think I'm ready to move on." Jane Ann looked around and watched the flashlight beams bouncing around in the hills. "It's hard to appreciate nature with all of this going on."

Finally they could see lights coming down out of the cliffs and watched the emerging group continue to the rescue unit.

They walked over, and Frannie was relieved to see the woman on the stretcher had an IV hooked up, and she wasn't zipped into a body bag—both good signs. The three boys, along with two girls, followed the sheriff. One of the girls wiped her eyes. The whole procession put Frannie in mind of one of the funeral parades in New Orleans. Except, of course, no one was dancing or playing an instrument.

Gus and Spider nodded at Mickey and the group. The sheriff visited briefly with the driver, and the rescue unit took off. He turned to the kids. "Can I give you a ride to your car? Or do you need me to explain to your parents where you've been?"

"We'll take a ride," Spider said. "But we left our backpacks with those people." He nodded toward the Ferraros.

"Okay, pick 'em up and come back here."

Gus and Spider walked back to the campsite with the Shoemakers and the Ferraros.

"So, do they think the woman is going to be okay? Or could you tell?" Frannie asked Gus.

"I think so. She got hit on the head. Our friend Kyra knows her. Her name is Lizzie or something and she's an archeologist—or used to be. Kyra thinks she would have had a backpack for sure." Gus seemed to be almost unburdening his soul. Stress does funny things to people.

"And there wasn't any backpack there?" Jane Ann asked.

"No!" said Spider. "Kyra says she hikes a lot and wouldn't be out without at least water."

"Very strange," said Frannie.

"I know, right?" Spider shook his head at the folly of it all. He picked up the packs and handed Gus his.

"Thanks for the snacks," Gus said. "We gotta go." The Shoemakers and Ferraros watched the boys walk back toward the sheriff's car.

The ranger returned to get his truck, started to get in, and then closed the door and walked over the group, still chewing on his toothpick.

"Just wanted you to know we'll be closing off the hiking trails in this area for the next few days."

Frannie nodded and said, "The boys said that one of the girls knows the woman who was hurt?"

"Yeah, we know her too. She hikes out here a lot. As a matter of fact, she's the one who reported the other hiker this morning." He paused as if deciding what to say. "She said there was another man who had been trying to help the fallen hiker, but he was gone when we got back up there. She was afraid that he had hit his head and wandered off. I'm thinking now he may be the escapee, and he knocked her down to take her pack. That's why we're closing the trails. He's still out there somewhere, and he's dangerous."

"You mean she went looking for him?" Larry asked.

"I think so. We were busy getting the other hiker off the cliff, and she just disappeared. We assumed she continued her own hike." They all looked toward the campground entrance as lights flashed, and four patrol cars circled the sites on the gravel road, coming to a halt near the hiking trail. Uniformed officers emerged from all of the cars and switched on flashlights.

The ranger said, "Search party," and turned on his heel to join them. Again he came back and focused on Frannie.

"Ma'am, you said the hiker this morning was wearing a Kansas Jayhawks sweatshirt?"

"Yes, with a hood."

"What color was it?"

She thought a minute, picturing the hiker. "Grey with blue letters, I think. Didn't he have it on when you found him?"

He shook his head. "Just a T-shirt and your husband's raincoat. Better go. Thanks!" This time he loped down the road to the hiking trail.

The four looked at each other.

"Well," Jane Ann said. "Here we are again."

"At least we didn't find the body," Frannie said, and immediately regretted being so flippant about the young man's death.

Larry rubbed his hand across his head. "I still can't figure out how he got that raincoat."

"It apparently was the convict who found it and then exchanged with the hiker," Jane Ann said.

"But still..." Larry said.

"I wonder," Mickey said, and stared toward the lights of the search party moving up into the rocks.

The other three looked at him, waiting.

A scraping noise came from behind Ferraros' camper. Frannie frowned and started to speak, Larry shushed her. Mickey picked up a spatula, brandishing it like a weapon, and Jane Ann got the giggles. She covered her mouth as more sounds came from the back.

A shape appeared around the corner—small, round and luminescent. Frannie saw it first and gave a gasp. The others turned toward where she was pointing just as she realized the sham.

A black sweat suit, topped by a large top-heavy lime-green glow-in-the-dark egg with big vacant eyes and a tiny mouth, screeched, "Boo!"

"Oh, man," Mickey said, "I saw those masks at the museum gift shop but I was afraid Jane Ann would just take it away."

"I would have — and thrown it in the trash," Jane Ann said.

"Did I scare you?" said the tiny mouth without moving.

"More than you know," Frannie said, her hand on her heart. "Are you camping nearby?"

The figure pointed toward the back of Ferraros' coach.

"Wif my mom and dad."

"Robbie!" A tall twenty-something man with tousled blonde hair rounded the corner behind the little alien. He looked at the group. "I'm really sorry. He's so excited about his mask."

"Well, he had us fooled," Mickey said. "We thought it was a real invasion."

"Actually, Mickey hoped that it was," Jane Ann said.

The young man laughed and held out his hand. "Name's Fred Putz. Don't laugh. Anyway, it's about his bedtime."

The alien reluctantly took his dad's hand, who led him back around the coach.

"What were you wondering, Mick?" Larry said.

Mickey turned back from watching the pair. "What?"

"Before your little friend found you. You said 'I wonder.'"

Mickey looked genuinely perplexed. "What were we talking about?"

"How my raincoat ended up on a dead hiker."

"Oh!" Mickey leaned forward in his chair, resting his elbows on his knees. "What if the convict—Badger, or whatever his name is—escaped at that gas station we stopped at and saw you put that rain suit in there. If you didn't lock the hatch, he could have taken it before we ever left Artesia."

"Or," Frannie felt a numbing chill, "He could have crawled in the cubby himself and rode here with us."

"That would explain a lot," Jane Ann said.

Larry looked at his wife with admiration. "It would explain everything. We need to tell the sheriff—they should check that compartment for fingerprints and other evidence. Good thinking, Fran."

"Not much good about it," she said. "I thought it was spooky that he may have just taken something out of that compartment. If he was actually in there, he must have been there when we went to bed last night and snuck out while we were asleep and that is *really* creepy." She thought a moment more. "He had to get out from the inside because you didn't unlock that hatch until this morning."

"Right. So the sheriff was right—we did help him, except we didn't know it."

Frannie sat forward in her chair. "Larry! There's a knife missing from knife block behind the stove! I assumed you had put it in a drawer last time you dried dishes. Do you remember?"

"That was the last night in Texas, right?" He shook his head. "Doesn't matter. If there's an empty slot in the block, I always put them in there."

"So he might have taken a knife from us, too." Frannie looked up toward the hills.

"But he hasn't used it yet," Mickey said. "At least it sounds like both of the victims today were hit with something. They didn't mention any stabbing."

"Noo—but if they got hit with something, maybe it was the crosspiece from our grill." Larry got up. "I'll go see if there's someone who can report this to the sheriff. There's probably someone manning the radio and coordinating the search."

CHAPTER NINE
WEDNESDAY NIGHT

BADGER WAS MORE DETERMINED than ever to get away from the hellhole that he was in. With two more bodies in his wake, the manhunt for him would expand and intensify. He stopped a moment, hefted the strap of the pack to a more comfortable spot, and glanced up at the sky. Instead of heading east toward the desert, he would go north along this ridge of rock. He decided he had a better chance if he stayed within reasonable distance of civilization and the supplies and transportation he needed. Even if he could get hold of DeWayne, his old buddy was probably too far away to help in time.

He needed a hideout where he could lay low until the search fizzled out. Then maybe he *should* go to Mexico. He shook his head as he continued in what he thought was a northerly direction. He could deal with that later. He needed to stay alert and get as far as he could now that he had some supplies.

He walked for about an hour, only having to veer off course once to avoid a group of hikers. After climbing down into a draw and back up the other side, he paused in a nook to rest and take stock of the contents of the backpack.

There were three more bottles of water in addition to the empty one the old lady had taken back from him. He threw that one away and watched it roll down the rocky hillside into the draw. He opened another bottle and took a few sips, closing it and returning it to the pack. He congratulated himself on his new-found prudence. Not that he wasn't thirsty; with the bouts of fever and chills, he could have downed a gallon of water in one sitting. He had to be smart like a fox, if he was going to get away. And he could do that.

In a pocket were four granola bars. An orange and an apple rolled around loose in the bag. A small first aid kit reminded him of his injured hand. He found some antiseptic cream in the kit and smeared some on the snakebite. A small notebook and pen didn't promise much use but he would keep them anyway — didn't weigh much. In another pocket was a billfold. A couple of credit cards might be useful, but not as much as a wad of cash. He counted it — one hundred and thirty-seven dollars. This was a gold mine to Badger. He didn't need a lot of money, but cash was always good. He had hoped to find a cell phone in one of the pockets but no such luck.

He took a couple of bites of one of the granola bars and carefully folded the foil wrapper back around it. Slinging the pack over his other shoulder, he resumed his journey, feeling a little more in control of his situation.

He stopped every hour or hour and a half, near as he could tell. Rocky climbs and treacherous slopes with loose gravel challenged him. But he had spent hours on the prison treadmill and working out with weights so he was no wimp. A couple of sips of water, another bite of the granola bar, a short rest, and on his way again. Sometimes the shakes would take him, and he just wanted to curl up in a ball. But he didn't. With each stop, he was more certain that they would never catch him.

But as the afternoon wore on, he wasn't so sure. The scenery never changed, and he felt like he was making no progress. It seemed like he'd passed the same rocks and taken the same turns several times.

Badger thought about spending the night in the rocks with half the cops in the county looking for him. He sat down on a flat rock, checking around first to make sure there were no snakes nearby, and went through his options again as he finished off a granola bar.

He wasn't getting anywhere. Even if he got to a highway or town, then what? He needed a ride, and he needed to find it tonight somewhere where they wouldn't be looking for him. Not a highway.

A new idea began to creep into his muddled mind. He checked the direction of the sun and headed back that way. As it got darker, lights briefly flashed off of rocky towers and cliff sides. Searchers. They wouldn't be looking for him back at the campground. And there were trucks and RVs there. He could steal a truck. Or an RV — not one of those trailers, but the kind you drive. Pick up a hostage or two that would get him out of the state. Now he had a plan again. He walked toward the western edge of the rocky hills. It was full dark by the time he reached the little valley. He could see the lights of the campground to the south. For all his wandering, he hadn't traveled very far.

Moving more cautiously, he worked his way through the tree and brush line below the cliffs until he reached the campground area. He found a clump of tall shrubs with an open area in the center. A perfect hiding spot to watch the campground from. He sat down to wait. The stubby trees were nothing like the tall pines of the Wisconsin woods where his foster dad used to make him hide when the social workers came around. He remembered too well one long night that he spent trembling in fear of bears and other wildlife. Tonight, the occasional howl of a coyote and rustling in the scrubby grass did nothing to relax him.

He just needed a couple more lucky breaks.

BY THE TIME lights had blinked out in most of the campers, Badger was stiff from trying to avoid moving or making noise, and his hand hurt. He hadn't seen any of the searchers' lights at this end of the park, so he took a chance, and stood up carefully to stretch. He needed to wait still longer, to give people time to get to sleep. A thin moon rode high in the sky, giving very little light.

He broke open another granola bar, ate the apple, and downed most of a bottle of water. By that time, he felt safe in moving to the end of the nearest row of campers. He had decided while he waited that he would just try the motorhomes and not the trucks. Too many cars and trucks had alarm systems, but he didn't think they were very common on campers. Slowly and silently, he tried the door on the first one. It was locked. He continued to the next, and the next, until he found a door that opened.

He looked around to be sure he wasn't being watched, and eased the door open. Then he listened to the silent interior before edging his way up the steps. No jerky moves; nothing that would make the camper bounce.

Once inside, he closed the door and gently released the latch. He straightened up and looked around. Since his eyes were already accustomed to the dark, it wasn't hard to make out shapes. A counter of some sort was to his left, and a table with benches was silhouetted against the window across from him. He turned to the right and realized that he could hear heavy breathing at the same time that he spotted lumpy forms on an open couch.

He pulled the knife out of his sweatshirt pocket and bent closer to the forms, holding his breath. The head nearest him had long, light hair splayed across the pillow. Excellent. The wife.

As he positioned the knife near her throat, she moved and mumbled in her sleep.

"Don't scream, lady, and you'll be fine," he whispered.

Her eyes flew open and her face froze in terror.

"Wha — ?"

"I said be quiet!"

The man on the other side of the bed rolled over, but continued snoring.

"Get up!" he whispered and kept the knife near her throat, as she got to a sitting position. Her eyes were wide, and she crossed her arms over her chest, clutching her shoulders.

"Can you drive this thing?" Badger nodded toward the driver's seat of the coach.

The woman shook her head.

"Get your husband up then. Don't try anything funny —this knife will be right at your back."

She leaned over and shook the man's shoulder.

"Mickey! Wake up." She glanced back over her shoulder at Badger. "And don't yell."

Mickey opened his eyes, confused and then focused in on Badger and his wife. "What the hell is going on?"

She put a hand on his chest. "Shhh—he's got a knife on me."

"And I'll use it if you try anything funny. Get up. You're going to drive us out of here."

Mickey pushed himself up to sitting. "Drive us where?"

Badger grabbed Jane Ann around the waist with one arm and held the knife at her throat with the other. "Now!" He was losing patience.

Mickey scooted across the foldout bed to the narrow aisle. Badger pulled Jane Ann back toward the kitchen area both to give him room to get up and prevent any stupid heroics.

Mickey pulled a sweatshirt on over his flannel pajamas and reached under the bed.

"Hold it!" Badger said. His whisper was becoming hoarse from the strain of trying to keep his voice down. "What are you doing?"

Mickey stood and held up a pair of tennis shoes. "Just getting these. Honest." He concentrated on Jane Ann's face, trying to reassure her.

"All right. Make it quick."

Mickey sat on the edge of the bed to put his shoes on, looking up frequently to check on Badger.

"What do you have to do to get this thing out of here?"

"I have to unplug it and take the wheel chocks out. We aren't hooked up to water." Mickey's voice was shaking.

Badger motioned Mickey ahead of him toward the door. "Do it. Quietly."

Mickey opened the door, went down the steps, and started to close it. Badger pushed Jane Ann ahead and said in a low growl, "We'll be right behind you."

Mickey pulled the wheel brakes out and went around to the post to unplug and stow the cord. Badger followed him and made sure Mickey could see the knife every time he looked at them. In spite of the chilly air, sweat was running down Mickey's face.

Mickey bent over and reached under the coach. "What're you doing?" Badger demanded.

"Uh—just checking the wires. Sometimes they hang down and make sparks on the road.

Badger nodded. "Okay. Get back inside."

Mickey led the way and Badger closed the door firmly behind them. He motioned Mickey to the driver's seat and Jane Ann to the passenger seat. He perched behind her on the end of the couch with the knife at the back of her neck.

"Okay, buddy, get this thing back to the highway. Don't try *anything* cute. You might think you can get away with it, but are you don't want to piss me off."

"No. No, I'm not trying anything," Mickey said quietly.

"Let's go."

Mickey started the engine and began to slowly back out. Fortunately, there weren't any campers in the sites across the road so he had ample room to maneuver in the dark. The coach was quiet as they bumped their way up the entrance road to the highway.

"Turn right," Badger said, when they got to the stop sign.

CHAPTER TEN
THURSDAY MORNING

FRANNIE SLEPT LATER than usual the next morning. By the time the coffee had perked and she headed outside with her blanket and mug, the sun was just edging over the red rock hills to the east. She dragged her lawn chair to face the hills but stopped as her brain registered the empty spot next door.

She just stood there and stared. Mickey and Jane Ann's camper was gone. She couldn't wrap her mind around it. Never in all of the years they had camped together had anyone just left in the middle of the night. What could have made them move? If their power post had failed, their furnace would still run, and what else would they need? She couldn't think of any other reason they would move. She set her coffee on the picnic table and hurried toward the road.

She scanned the part of the campground she could see. Although there were several empty sites, Mickey and Jane Ann's class C Lazy Daze motorhome, affectionately called the Red Rocket for its distinctive paint scheme, was nowhere to be seen.

She rushed back into her own trailer and called to Larry as she headed to the bedroom. He stirred, and she shook his shoulder.

"Larry! Wake up. Mickey and Jane Ann are gone!"

He opened his eyes and squinted at her. "What are you talking about?" He leaned over and peered at the little clock on his nightstand. "Where'd they go?"

"That's just it. I don't know! Their camper is gone too." She thought a moment. "But their lawn chairs are still sitting where they were last night. Something's happened to them."

He sat up and rubbed an eye with the heel of his hand. She wanted to shake him but knew he wasn't fully awake yet.

"Gone? The Rocket's gone too?"

"Yes! Get some clothes on. We've got to find the ranger or the sheriff."

She moved out of his way, so he could get dressed and went back outside, almost expecting to see the Rocket in its usual space. She would have gladly admitted to Larry that she was losing her mind. No such luck. Their spot was still empty.

She retrieved her coffee mug and sipped it while she walked around the gravel pad. The wheel brakes were lying on the ground. She noticed a darker spot in the middle. A wet trail led out of the site and then along the road toward the entrance.

The camper door slammed as Larry came out, still looking half asleep. He stood staring at the vacant site.

"What in the world —-?"

"They couldn't have left willingly," Frannie said. "They would have told us. They wouldn't have left this stuff — the wheel brakes, their chairs — look, even Mickey's favorite spatula." She picked it up off the ground by Mickey's chair. "And look over here. This is wet." She pointed to the spot in the gravel. "Mickey must have opened his water line."

"You think they were forced? By the convict?"

"What other explanation is there? Unless Mickey's aliens got him." She gave a wry smile.

Larry shook his head, as if trying to clear it. "I'm afraid you may be right. About the convict, not the aliens. We need to find the ranger and then see if we can follow that trail. Trust Mickey to use something that would evaporate."

"I'm going to get my purse and lock the trailer," Frannie said.

Larry followed her and filled a travel mug with coffee and unplugged the pot. "Try calling them. Probably won't do much good, but you never know." Larry rubbed his crew cut and looked at Frannie with the most hangdog expression she'd ever seen on him.

She found her phone in a basket by the TV — she was notorious for never carrying it — and turned around and gave him a hug. "We'll find her — them."

He nodded, but didn't look convinced. Of all of the Shoemaker siblings, Larry and Jane Ann were the closest, partly because they camped together so much. But they had bonded as children because, they always said, their older brother Bob had been too bossy and their baby sister Elaine too spoiled.

They locked up and climbed in the truck. Frannie punched Jane Ann's number and let it ring while Larry pointed the truck toward the guard shack at the entrance. The call went to voice mail.

A perky Jane Ann said, "Hi! This is Jane Ann. Can't talk right now, but I'll call you back ASAP if you leave your name and number at the beep." It gave Frannie a chill as she thought about the possible reason Jane Ann couldn't 'talk right now.' But she just said, "It's Frannie. Call me."

Then she hit Mickey's number, and got the same response, except the message was typical Mickey: "Hi. It's Mick. Did I call you or did you call me? You know the routine."

She looked at Larry and shook her head.

"I figured," he said. Larry pulled in at the guard shack. They both jumped out of the truck and hurried to the window.

"Is the ranger around?" Larry asked. He put his hand on the back of Frannie's neck and massaged it, trying to make himself feel better.

"Which one?"

"What? We've only seen one, but any will do."

"Bryce is on duty, but he's out in the park somewhere. Is it an emergency?" The guard, an older man, straightened papers and stacked them neatly on the ledge in front of him.

"Yes!" Larry said sharply, and then backed off. "Sorry, my sister and her husband are missing. Can you call the sheriff?"

He fumbled his stack of papers. "Oh! Missing, you say? I'd better call the sheriff." He lowered his voice. "There's an escaped convict running around here. We've had two people attacked and one of them..." He apparently caught the look of impatience on Larry's face and picked up the phone. "I'll call him."

After giving the sheriff the news, the guard handed the phone to Larry. "He wants to talk to you."

Larry gave the sheriff a description of the Ferraro motorhome, including the license number. He insisted there was no other reason they could think of for Mickey and Jane Ann leaving in the middle of the night without telling them, and listened a minute, then said "Okay." He passed the phone back to the guard and turned to Frannie.

"He wants us to meet him out at the highway entrance to the park."

As they loped back to the truck, Frannie called "Thank you!" over her shoulder to the guard and barely boosted herself back into the pickup before Larry had it moving.

When they reached the entrance, Larry let the motor idle and sat drumming his fingers on the steering wheel. He craned his neck left and right, watching for the sheriff along the highway. Once looking right, he pointed out the window to Frannie.

"A trail of water going that way — very faint — see it? They must have gone north."

A siren preceded the sheriff's cruiser topping the hill in the same direction. Larry got out of the truck to wait for him. The sheriff pulled off on to the gravel, skidded to a halt, and rolled down his window. Frannie leaned over to hear the conversation.

"I think they went north. Mickey left his water line open, and there's still a faint trail going that way." Larry pointed at the slightly darker line on the road to the north.

The sheriff scoffed and shook his head. "He's crazy if he doesn't head for Mexico. I sent the description of the camper to the border posts, but they may have already gotten through. You don't know how long they've been gone?"

"No — just sometime between 11:00 last night and 6:00 this morning. But I really think they went north."

"That water trail could be from anything. If it was left more than a few hours ago, it would have evaporated by now. I've notified the state patrol, but we're going to concentrate on the area south of here. Take my word — he'll head for Mexico. I got your report last night about him possibly being a stowaway in your camper. If he really got in your camper in Artesia, he wouldn't have known which way you were going. He was just trying to get out of town. Let me know if you hear anything. And give me your phone number."

Larry recited it as the sheriff punched it into his phone. "Can we get a direct number for you?" He motioned to Frannie to write it down as the sheriff dictated.

Larry took a step back as the sheriff began to roll up his window. "Thanks. Please stay in touch."

"Okay," the sheriff replied. He finished rolling up his window and peeled out to the south.

Larry came back to the truck, shaking his head. He got in and looked at Frannie. "I think we'll head north."

They both were wrapped up in their own thoughts the first few miles, and then Frannie pulled out the road atlas. She turned to the New Mexico page.

She pored over the map, finding their approximate location. "If they went this way, where do you suppose he's headed?"

Before Larry could say anything, his phone rang. He grabbed it off the dash, glanced at the screen, and groaned. He handed it to Frannie. "It's Mom. Don't tell her what's going on."

Frannie nodded and took the call.

"Larry?"

"No, Mom, this is Frannie. Larry's driving right now."

"Oh, hi, honey — how are you? Is everything okay?"

Frannie frowned. "Sure — um — everything's fine. Why?"

"I've been trying and trying to get Jane Ann, and she doesn't answer. I got worried."

"Maybe her phone's dead."

"But I've tried Mickey too, and he doesn't answer either."

"We've had trouble sometimes with reception here— we're in the middle of the desert. I don't think we have the same carrier so maybe that's why you can get us and not them. Is something wrong? I can give her a message." Frannie hoped lightning wouldn't strike her for lying to her mother-in-law.

"No—nothing's wrong. But you can tell her that Betsy Dawes is in town for a week or two. She was Jane Ann's best friend in high school and hasn't been back in years. I was hoping you'd be back in time for Jane Ann to see her."

"Oh, I see." Frannie relaxed a little. "I'll tell her when we stop. We'll talk it over and let you know when we plan to be home. Everyone okay there? How's Stan doing?"

She laughed. "Cranky as usual. But we're both fine. You kids have fun. Talk to you later."

She was gone. "When your mom decides to end a call, she ends a call."

"She still thinks she's paying by the minute. What did she want?"

Frannie explained about the visiting friend.

"Well, let's hope we can give her the message soon." He rubbed his hand over his crew cut. "I wouldn't think this guy would want to stay on a main road. The Rocket is too conspicuous. What roads does it show connecting to this one? There can't be many — we haven't passed any crossroads yet."

Frannie looked back at the map, and then her head popped up. "Remember last night Mickey said he had to be sure and gas up before we went too far today? I bet they would have stayed on the main road until they found a place to get gas — probably Roswell. Gas stations aren't exactly plentiful out here."

"That's right!" Larry brightened at the prospect of possibly narrowing down the route of the fugitive. "Okay, let's assume they would get gas in Roswell if not before. Check to see what roads go off of this highway after Roswell."

BADGER FELT HIMSELF getting feverish again. It was an effort to hold his hand and the knife still. No one spoke for several miles, and then Mickey did.

"Um, sir? We don't have much gas. I was going to fill it up before we headed out today."

Baxter rolled his eyes. Sounded like a trick to him. He leaned over to where he could see the gas gauge. It was almost on empty—so the guy wasn't lying. He thought a few moments.

"Okay, here's what we're going to do. We'll stop in Roswell—where I tell you and not before. No credit cards —I know they can trace those, so don't try and pull that. What do you have for cash?"

Mickey glanced at his wife. "I've got about fifty bucks is all. Jane Ann? You have any?"

"Only about twenty," she said, very softly.

"We could stop at an ATM," Mickey said.

"No! Just cuz I've been in prison doesn't mean I'm an idiot. I've got some money, so I want you to fill it up. We ain't gonna stop again any time soon." He didn't catch the look between Mickey and his wife.

Most of the landscape illuminated by the headlights was desert—brown, bare, sparse vegetation, flat. Occasionally an eruption of rock cliffs or a yawning gorge broke the monotony.

Badger took advantage of the silence to take quick glances at the comforts offered by the motorhome. This thing would be a piece of cake to drive—he really didn't need these people, especially once he was out of New Mexico. He could get a bunch of spray paint and paint the damn thing, pick up DeWayne in Wisconsin, and head for Canada. He drove a truck for a few months before he went to the joint. This wouldn't be any harder than that.

On the outskirts of Roswell, a few sad-looking businesses dotted the landscape like discarded toys. Weeds surrounded a boarded up cement block building. A crooked sign identified a struggling pawn shop. Sagging trailers were strewn back from the road. The eerie glow of scattered streetlights made them more desolate. Closer to town, a large, brightly-lighted truck stop sprouted multiple islands with gas pumps on two sides, rows of parked semis, and probably twenty or more passenger cars and pickups.

"Here?" Mickey asked.

"I'll tell you when," Badger said.

They passed another large station and a smaller one, but still with numerous customers. Finally, Badger spotted a gas station back away from the road. It didn't even have a convenience store attached and looked hungry for business. A lighted sign in the window said "OPE."

"Turn here," Badger said to Mickey. "Head for that station. Remember, no funny stuff." He moved the knife a little closer to Jane Ann's neck. Her eyes widened in fear as she tried to shrink back into the seat.

The station had one island with two pumps. Mickey pulled the motorhome next to the second pump and looked back at Badger who nodded. Mickey got out.

As he started to fill the tank, a skinny old man came out of the station and sat down in a rickety wooden chair, tipping back against the station window. The man watched Mickey with a fixed stare.

After what seemed like an eternity, Badger said to Jane Ann, "What's goin' on? Doesn't take that long to fill a tank."

"This one does," Jane Ann said.

Badger looked at the readout on the gas pump. "What's he doing? Dumping it on the ground? That's over a hundred and twenty dollars already!"

"This has a 45-gallon tank," Jane Ann said.

Badger was ready to scream at her but thought better of it and gritted his teeth. "Tell him to shut it off."

Jane Ann lowered the driver's window from her armrest. "Mickey, he says that's enough."

The old guy by the station tipped his chair forward and started to walk toward them. Badger thought about having Mickey drive off but didn't want to clue the cops in to what direction he had gone. He lowered the knife to

Jane Ann's side so the guy couldn't see it through the windshield, dug the wad of Lizzie Pryce's cash out of the backpack, and handed it to Mickey when he opened the door.

"Take care of it and make it quick."

The old man had rounded the front of the van. Mickey counted out the amount and handed to the old man. The man stayed in front of the vehicle while he examined some of the bills, nodded, and shuffled back to the station.

Mickey climbed back in and started the engine. "Now what?" he asked, without looking back.

"Drive. North."

They continued through Roswell. Traffic was just beginning to pick up as people on early shifts started their day. Very few cars were parked along the main street. When they reached the outskirts, Badger indicated to Jane Ann to get out the atlas stuck alongside the seat.

"I wanna get the hell out of New Mexico fast on back roads. So we're going to take the first road to the right." He peered over Jane Ann's shoulder. "Where's Roswell on that map?"

She pointed. "Interstate 70 is the next road to the east." She shifted a little, as he literally breathed down her neck.

"No Interstates. Find a back road — what's that?"

They all spotted the flashing blue and red lights ahead on the road at the same time.

"Looks like someone got pulled over for speeding," Mickey said. "They won't notice us."

"Unless they are already looking for us," Badger growled. "Turn on that road coming up."

"But that's going west—" Mickey said.

"Do what I say!" Badger brandished the knife near Jane Ann's neck. Mickey whipped the wheel and turned left on to a gravel road. He grimaced as he did so.

"He doesn't like to drive this coach on gravel," Jane Ann said quietly.

"Tough," Badger said. "This ain't about him." He grinned.

They bounced along, and Jane Ann kept a wary eye on the knife as it bounced too.

"I don't think this is going to take us anywhere," Mickey said. "Maybe one of the UFO crash sites."

"One of the what?"

"This is where the UFOs crashed back in the 40s, you know?"

Badger shook his head. "You believe in that stuff?"

Mickey kept a straight face. "There's a lot of evidence to support it."

Badger frowned. Just his luck to carjack a couple of nuts. "Whatever. When you get somewhere we can turn around, do that and pull over. We'll wait about ten or fifteen minutes, and then the cop should be gone."

Mickey nodded and continued down the rough road, flinching each time the coach hit a pothole. The flat, scrubby desert morphed into boulder-strewn mounds and rocky prominences. A large pullout on the right led to a driveway or road that disappeared between the rocks. Mickey maneuvered the coach into the space and aimed it back at the road. He looked at Badger.

"Just sit tight. I'll tell you when." He looked at the clock on the dash.

As they sat, the sky began to lighten and the stars faded. A howl came from the rocks to their right where a coyote perched and drew out his commentary on the world.

A crack against Mickey's window made them all jump. They turned away from the coyote to stare at the muzzle of a shotgun.

"Get out of here!" Badger yelled, and Mickey threw the motorhome into gear and gunned it. But the squeal of the tires and the rattle of thrown gravel did not cover up the blast of the gun. The coach lurched to the driver's side and settled at a cockeyed angle.

Mickey's eyes were wide. "She shot one of the tires out!"

"She?!?" Jane Ann's surprise made her temporarily forget her own precarious situation.

In answer to her question, a husky, middle-aged woman wearing jeans under a flowered cotton skirt, a fleece-lined denim jacket and a beat-up cowboy hat moved around to the front of the coach, the shotgun aimed at the windshield.

Badger stared at their assailant, his mouth half-open. How could an escape that started out so great go so wrong? "Now what?"

Mickey shrugged. "We can't go anywhere. We better see what she wants, dontcha think?" He looked back at Badger.

The convict just nodded. He needed to get back in control of this situation.

Mickey rolled down his window, luckily not broken by the strike from the shotgun. He barely stuck his head out and called to the woman. "Ma'am?"

"Yer on my land!" she yelled back.

"We'd like to leave," Mickey said, "but I'll have to change the tire first."

"Shouldn't have turned in here. Sign sez 'PRIVATE.'"

"We didn't see the sign. But now, we have to change the tire before we can leave."

The woman narrowed her eyes and peered in the windshield. "How many of ya in there?"

"Two besides me," Mickey said.

The woman waved the muzzle of the gun. "You get out. The other two stay in there. No funny stuff. Do you work for the government?"

"What? No." Mickey shook his head as he descended from the coach.

The woman watched him closely but yelled in the open window, "On second thought, you two get out here."

Jane Ann looked back at Badger and raised her eyebrows. He looked out at the woman with the shotgun. He nodded to Jane Ann.

"Get out slowly. I'll be gettin' out at the same time. She won't be able to see us behind the door. So's if you pull anything, I will hurt you, even if she gets me."

Jane Ann opened her door and slid out. Badger maneuvered between the seats and followed her closely, the knife prodding her as a reminder.

"Over here where I can see you," the woman said. Badger directed Jane Ann ahead of him with the tip of the knife around the front of the motorhome.

The woman glared at them. "You two stay there while he changes the tire, and then I want you all to get the hell out."

Jane Ann eyed her husband, who was pulling a toolbox out of a compartment. "Can I please help him? He has health problems. and we usually call a road service when we have a flat."

The woman squinted at her. "You sure you don't work for the government, comin' out here to snoop?"

"No! We're retired—I was a nurse and he was an English teacher."

"Let me see some ID."

Mickey stood up and pulled his billfold out of his back pocket with one hand while keeping the other one raised.

"My purse is in the RV," Jane Ann said.

"Stay there. I'll check his first." The woman reached for Mickey's open billfold. She kept the gun trained on them and handed the billfold back to Mickey. "Pull the rest of that stuff out and let me see it."

Mickey had regained a little color in his face. He pulled the rest of the cards out of the slot and fanned through them. "Library card, blood donor, AARP, teaching certificate..."

"What's that one?" She pointed to one peeking out of the back of the stack with a green head on it.

Mickey flushed a little. "Um..I joined the Friends of the UFO Museum yesterday..."

Jane Ann rolled her eyes in exasperation. "For God's sake, Mick..."

"Shut up," the woman said and cocked her head at Mickey. "You might be okay..." She turned to Jane Ann. "Now yours."

Jane Ann opened the passenger door and reached into her purse on the floor for her billfold. As she did, her hand brushed her phone, and she turned it on and tried by feel to push the button for Larry's speed dial. She straightened and held up the billfold for the woman to see.

"Show me."

Jane Ann pulled out her license and a couple of other cards and held them out to the woman.

Badger started to move around Jane Ann toward the woman. This had gone on long enough and he was still stuck in New Mexico. But she caught the movement and as she did, her eyes fixed on the knife in his hand.

"What the hell?" she said, and fired.

CHAPTER TWELVE
THURSDAY MORNING

FRANNIE SAT FORWARD, scanning the road ahead of them and the desolate landscape along the roadside.

Larry pounded a fist on the steering wheel. He too was leaning forward, as if that would bring him closer to the Ferraros.

"What?" Frannie said, alarmed that a new problem had added to their mountainous pile.

He shook his head. "Just that if I had locked that damn compartment, this wouldn't be happening."

"Maybe not, but you don't know what the guy would have done then. Maybe he would have attacked us or Jane Ann and Mickey to get our vehicles."

"Do we have any pictures with us that show the Rocket?" Larry asked.

"No... there's some in my scrapbooks in the camper."

"Damn. Wish I'd thought of it before we left."

"Wait!" Frannie picked up her phone and scrolled through the photos. "I took one of them by that huge cactus a couple of days ago. Part of the Rocket should show in it. Here it is!" She held it up.

He glanced over at it. "That'll help. Keep it handy — I'm going to stop at some of the gas stations and see if anyone remembers them. You know, if Mom calls again, don't answer. Let her think we aren't getting a signal. Otherwise, she'll catch on that something's wrong."

Frannie nodded. The reality of the situation began to overwhelm her. Something was certainly wrong. She began to tear up as she thought of the laughter, the worries, and the mundane everyday events that she and Jane Ann had shared over the years. And Mickey — would Mickey stop being a clown long enough not to rile up a convicted murderer? Her gut seized up at the thought of anything bad happening to either one of them.

As they neared Roswell, Larry stopped at a large truck stop. He parked in front of the convenience store and said to Frannie, "Bring your phone." She pulled up the photo again as they hurried into the store.

The store swarmed with morning commuters and travelers filling their coffee mugs and stocking up on snacks. Larry grabbed Frannie's phone and stepped up to the counter ahead of a portly man with a travel mug and large bag of chips.

"Hey!" the guy said.

Larry held up a hand.

"Please — it's an emergency. I just need to ask a question."

The man sputtered but gave a few inches. The clerk, a college-aged boy with thick glasses, looked at Larry like he had dropped from a UFO.

"Have you seen this motorhome or these people come in here this morning?"

The boy looked at the phone. "Don't think so."

"Okay, thanks — sorry," Larry said to the man with the chips.

They hurried back to the truck.

The next stop produced the same results. At the third station, the middle-aged clerk shook her head at the picture on the phone, but a young woman bouncing a toddler on her hip craned her neck to look at the photo as Larry was showing it to the clerk and said "I think I saw that RV go through town earlier! Never seen one like it before, and we're big campers."

"Really? What direction was it going? When did you see it?"

"It was goin' north. We live right on the highway and I was just taking the baby out for a walk. A couple of hours ago." She rubbed the baby's back, as he started to fuss.

Larry said, "You're pretty sure it was this RV?"

"*Pretty* sure — sorry, I can't be more help. Was it stolen?"

"You might say that. Thanks so much!" Larry pushed Frannie ahead of him out the door.

"At least we know which way they're going," Frannie said.

"She said *pretty* sure...but it is certainly distinctive." Larry pulled back out on the highway, continuing north. "I just wish I knew if this Badger guy would want to stop at busy places because they would be lost in a crowd but take a chance on being seen by more people or in isolated spots but where they might stand out more."

Frannie pointed. "There's certainly an isolated one if you want to check it out." The small old station sat back from the road with no customers. Larry turned sharply into the side street leading to the station and Frannie hung on to the handhold.

As Frannie got out, she shed the heavier jacket she had put on against the early morning chill and followed Larry into the station. This was not the usual full-service convenience store; the few dusty packets of peanuts and chips clipped to a wire stand on the counter looked like they predated the millennium.

An old man leaned back in a desk chair behind the counter, feet up on a plastic bucket and reading the *Wall Street Journal*. Frannie thought what a great incongruous photo it would make.

"Yeah?" he said, looking up from his paper but not abandoning his comfortable position.

Larry held out the phone with the photo. "We're looking for these people and this motorhome. We think they may have stopped for gas somewhere along here."

"Yeah?" the man said again.

Larry held his impatience. "Have you seen them?"

The man put his paper down and leaned forward to peer more closely at the photo.

"Yeah."

Larry perked up. "You did?"

"I said I did."

"How long ago? Did they buy gas?"

"Yup. Paid cash. Not many people carry that much cash but fine with me."

Frannie was watching him, barely breathing. She glanced to her right at a bulletin board thick with notices and sale announcements. Many were yellowed and curled, but right in the middle was a crisp copy of a wanted poster with Baxter Bagley's photo on it.

She poked the poster with her index finger. "Was this guy with them?"

"I dunno. I talked to that guy." He pointed at Mickey on Frannie's phone. "He filled the tank. He paid the money."

Larry took a deep breath. "Well, was there anyone else in the RV, could you tell?"

"Mebbe. Mighta been a woman in the passenger seat. Didn't really notice." He peered over at the poster, as if the question just registered with him. "You mean that convict mighta been in there?"

"Probably."

"Say, you a cop?"

"Not any more," Larry said. "But that woman is my sister. So, how long ago was this?"

The old man glanced at the dusty "Dad's Old Fashioned Root Beer" clock on the wall.

"I'd say about two and a half hours ago."

"Okay. One more question. Do you know which way they went?"

"North."

"You're sure?"

"Haven't had any more customers since then."

Larry grabbed Frannie's hand. "Thank you very much." He pulled her toward the door.

"Dontcha want any gas or anything?" the old man called after them, but they didn't respond.

"Talk about pulling teeth, " Larry muttered, as they climbed back in the truck. "Well, there's no doubt in my mind that it's them, and we're on the right track." He handed Frannie her phone back. "Call the sheriff and put it on speaker, please. I hope we can convince him—wait! First write down the name and address of this station."

He read the name and street number off to her before he pulled out on the street, and she copied it down on the console notepad. Then she punched in the number she'd written down earlier. While it was ringing, she switched on the speaker and laid the phone on the console between them.

"Parsons," came the gruff voice.

"Sheriff, this is Larry Shoemaker, from the campground? It was my sister who was abducted this morning?"

A slight pause. "Yes, Mr. Shoemaker."

"We're up here in Roswell—my brother-in-law said last night he needed to get gas right away this morning, so we've been checking gas stations. We just found the one they stopped at. Geezer's Gasser on Sixth Street."

"How do you know it was them and not some other RV?" The skepticism was heavy in the sheriff's voice.

"I showed him a photo on my wife's phone. He identified the RV and my brother-in-law."

"I don't know why they'd go north," the sheriff said.

"I don't either, but I'm sure they did."

A loud sigh drifted from the phone. "Okay. I'll let my men know. We've got the staties involved now, too. Can you send me that photo?"

"Yes," Frannie said. "I'll do that."

Larry looked over at Frannie as the phone clicked off. "He's still not convinced." He pulled the truck back out onto the street and then turned north again at the highway.

"So now what?" Frannie asked.

"We're going to keep going. Even if the sheriff does redirect the search, it'll take 'em a while to get back up here."

They continued through downtown Roswell, now busy with morning traffic. The lift of having their route confirmed dissipated as Frannie pored over the map and realized the multitude of options.

"Two and a half hours—they could be in Texas or near Santa Fe or who knows?" But when she saw Larry's face and the discouragement there, she added, "But we won't be the only ones looking, and it's hard to miss the Rocket. Surely the sheriff has put out bulletins?"

"I'm sure he has. You started to check earlier on roads going off this highway. What do you see there?"

"Interstate 70 goes northeast right on the north edge of town."

"I still think he'll go for back roads, now that they have gas."

"There's a 246 that heads northwest also on the north edge of town. Nothing else going east until Highway 20 several miles north. Of course this doesn't show any county roads."

"They're probably not as frequent as in Iowa, but there have to be some. Well, we'll just have to use our best guess as we come to them. You seem to think he'd want to go east. Why?

Frannie shrugged. "I really don't know, except it's the shortest distance to a state line, and I would think he feel a little safer out of the state. And he's from Wisconsin, so if he's not trying to get to Mexico, maybe he's headed home."

"As good a guess as any. We probably should make a bathroom stop and at least pick up some bottles of water before we leave town. Never thought of it at those stations we already stopped at."

"You do have other things on your mind."

A few minutes later, they stopped at another convenience store and soon, stocked with coffee, bottles of water, and a few granola bars, were back on the road.

CHAPTER THIRTEEN

THURSDAY AFTERNOON

JANE ANN SCREAMED and dived for the motorhome. Badger stood his ground, but dropped the knife in reaction to the blast. The woman had fired just past him into the surrounding rock. When he bent to retrieve the knife, she said, "Don't move."

He straightened and looked her in eyes, waiting.

"What's going on here?" she demanded.

"Just trying to defend myself," Badger said. "Nuthin' wrong with that."

Mickey, on the other side of the motorhome, had also taken cover as best he could but now stood up.

"He took us hostage. He's an escaped convict. He was holding that knife on my wife. We need to call the police."

"No!" the woman shouted. "Don't want no cops here!"

Badger relaxed and started to reach for the knife again.

The woman swung the muzzle of the gun back at him. "I *said* don't move. We got our own law enforcement here, and this is it." She waggled the gun slightly. "Y'all walk ahead a me. We're goin' back to the ranch to sort this out. That way." She motioned them toward the disappearing lane.

Mickey went first, followed by Jane Ann and Badger. The lane twisted around the rocks and down into a gorge. Jane Ann stepped carefully, trying to avoid a sprained ankle or worse. At the bottom of the gorge, a rambling structure sat surrounded by small buildings, fences and green patches. Smoke drifted up from the chimney, and a few people went about their tasks.

Faces turned up as they neared and spotted the woman brandishing the gun at her captives. No one looked alarmed. They all wore jeans, although the women wore loose flowing shirts that reached to their knees and most had on heavier jackets. As they were pushed along, Jane Ann examined the buildings for signs or some indication of where they were. A rough carving of a planet with rings topped the door of the biggest building, but that was about it.

The woman spoke to a young man working in a garden patch. "Tobiah, come with me. We need to confine these people, until we figure out what they're doing here." She directed them to one of the outlying sheds.

Inside the shed, only one small window let in any light, and they stumbled on the rough floor as their eyes adjusted to the dimness. The wall studs were exposed, and a variety of tools hung from nails around the room. Dust in the air caught at Jane Ann's throat, and she cringed at what appeared to be an old snakeskin crumpled along the wall.

The woman grabbed a coil of rope hanging on the wall and tossed it to Tobiah.

"Each of you take a chair. Tie that guy up first." She indicated Badger.

"Can you tell us where we are?" Mickey asked. He was looking pale and spent, and Jane Ann worried about his heart.

"Mickey, sit down," she said. "You look like you're about to drop."

His shoulders drooped, and he fell, more than sat, in the chair.

The woman continued to brandish the gun but seemed slightly less threatening. She waited until Tobiah had tied each of their hands behind the chairs.

"Now, what are you doing here, if you're not from the government?"

Mickey perked up and said, "He kidnapped us and forced us to drive him here."

Tobiah said to the woman, "Maranatha, do you want me to call the Council?"

"Not yet!" she snapped. She turned to Badger. "Who do *you* work for?'

The question caught him off guard. He couldn't remember the last time anyone had asked him where he worked. "What? I don't work for nobody."

"He just escaped from prison," Jane Ann said. "He murdered at least one person."

"The sheriff and the state cops are looking for him everywhere," Mickey said.

Maranatha jerked her head around at that. "Tobiah, you need to get that motor home out of sight. Now."

Mickey strained at his bonds as he watched Tobiah hurry out the door, slamming it behind him. "What do you mean?"

She sat on a bench by the door and kept the gun aimed at Badger. "We don't want the government here—anyone from the government."

Badger was sweating and he fidgeted in his chair. "Hey, lady, I don't like the gover'mint either. Let me go, and no way I'll report ya or bring anyone back here."

Maranatha shook her head. "We don't recognize the laws of the Interim Government, but we don't approve of murder either. We'll deal with you ourselves." There was a subtle menace in the statement.

Badger paled and started to reply but hesitated at a slight shift of the gun. Maranatha narrowed her eyes and swept them with a glance that said she was tired of talking. They sat in silence. Each of the prisoners occasionally tried to subtly find a more comfortable position and received a frown for the effort.

TOBIAH RECRUITED A teenaged boy, Eli, to help him with the motorhome. As they walked to the road, Tobiah said, "I don't know how big this is but if we have to tow it, I don't know if any of the ranch pickups will handle it."

Eli scuffed the dust of the lane as they walked. "What happened to it? Why are those people here?"

"Maranatha didn't say."

When they reached the coach, they walked around it, and Eli was the first to spot the tire.

"Looks like it's been shot!"

Tobiah gave a grim smile. "It doesn't surprise me. Maranatha doesn't think before..." He didn't finish his thought as he caught Eli's shocked look. "Don't matter. There's some tools here, but we're going to need a couple of jacks. I don't know how to work that one. C'mon — we'll get what we need, and then we won't have to tow it." They headed back to the ranch.

While they were gone, a rusty, battered pickup rattled along the road. It stopped shortly after it passed the lane and two young men got out. They searched the surrounding rocks with their eyes and walked around the motorhome.

One said, "It's unlocked!" and opened the driver's side door. He looked around the front of the coach and reached in and pulled out a purse. "Woohoo! This is our lucky day!" They high-fived each other.

"Someone's coming!" the second one warned.

The first one shut the door as quietly as he could, and the two took off in a lope toward their truck, purse in hand.

WHEN TOBIAH RETURNED to the shed, Maranatha stood up and turned to him. "Put the murderer in the snake pit."

That got Badger's attention. He yelled, "Snake pit! You can't do that! I already got bit yesterday!" He struggled to show them his arm, but Tobiah kept a grip on Badger's wrists with one large hand while he untied the rope with the other.

"Don't worry. We don't have snakes around here very often. It's just a name."

Jane Ann thought about the skin. Right.

Maranatha nudged Badger's shoulder with the muzzle of the gun. "Tobiah, did I ask you to talk?"

He looked up surprised. "No..." He stuttered a little. "Sorry, ma'am."

"This man is a murderer they said. He can stay in the snake pit, until we decide what do with him."

Tobiah nodded and did not reply. When Badger was loose, Tobiah retied his hands behind his back and pulled him by the arm toward the door. Badger yelled the whole time about his rights. His protests were still audible after the door slammed.

Mickey took a deep breath. "Ma'am, we are not from the government. We just want to fix our flat tire and get back to camping with our friends."

"We'll see about that," she said, and followed Tobiah out the door.

"That didn't sound especially promising," Jane Ann said.

Mickey shook his head and looked at his wife. The creases around his mouth, that usually crinkled upward in his mischievous smile, drooped. "I think we were better off on the road with a felon. That's where the cops will be looking. You got any ideas what this place is about?"

"I saw a planet carved above a doorway. That woman, Maranatha, seemed kind of impressed by your membership card for the UFO museum. So I'm guessing it's some kind of UFO group. But she made it clear that she didn't want any kind of authorities here, so I don't know if she'll let us go or not." She tried to block any thoughts of what not might mean.

"They probably wrecked the Rocket trying to move it," Mickey said glumly, "so even if they let us go, how will we ever get back to civilization?"

"When I got my billfold out of my purse, I tried to speed dial Larry, but I don't know if I hit the right button. Can they track us through our phones?"

"They do on TV."

"Well, then we know it's true, don't we?"

Mickey grimaced. "This is no time for sarcasm, dear." He straightened up as much as he could. "I think my phone's in my pocket. Can't get to it, though."

Jane Ann blew some hair out of her face. "This is kind of 'out of the frying pan into the fire,' isn't it?"

"Maybe the other way around—from the fire into the frying pan, but still in the hot seat."

The shed door creaked open, and a young woman stuck her head in.

"I brought you some water," she said. Like the other women they had seen outside, she wore jeans and a loose purple and blue print blouse, knee length with long sleeves and a high neck. Her dark hair was pulled back in a tight bun and she wore no makeup. She carried a bucket and a long handled dipper.

While the woman held the ladle up for Mickey to drink, Jane Ann said "Thank you. What is your name?"

The woman lowered her eyes. "Selah."

"Can you tell us what this place is?"

Selah brought the bucket over to Jane Ann and offered her a drink.

"Our place is called Preparation. We are the Church of Celestial Salvation Defenders. We believe that The Others will return for us before the end of the world."

"Like Heaven's Gate?" Mickey asked, his eyes wide.

"No. We don't know when it will happen—no one does. We just want to stay prepared and pass that on to our children for whenever it does happen."

She straightened and picked the bucket off the floor.

"Will they let us go? Why would they want to hold us? We were kidnapped by the other man," Jane Ann said.

"That's not for me to say," Selah said simply and left.

CHAPTER FOURTEEN
THURSDAY AFTERNOON

LARRY SLOWED THE TRUCK at each road branching off to the east. The first two showed no evidence of recent traffic, if the weeds growing in the gravel meant anything. Shortly afterwards, a helicopter passed over them going north.

"Is that the Highway Patrol?" Larry asked.

Frannie leaned forward and tried to peer up through the top of the windshield. "I can't tell. It looks like an 'SP' at the end of the number."

"Probably for State Police.   I wish—" He was interrupted by his cell phone. Frannie picked it up and looked at the screen. "The sheriff," she said, as she answered and put it on speaker.

"Mrs. Shoemaker?"

"Yes, but I have you on speaker. My husband's driving."

"Ah, yes. We're starting to move the search north of Roswell. Have you seen anything?"

"Not yet," Larry said. "We just saw a chopper go overhead—State Police maybe?"

"Probably. We've put a trace on their cell phones—should've done that sooner. They seem to be located northwest of Roswell. One of them's on the move, and the other isn't. I'll notify the chopper to head over that way."

Larry had abruptly pulled over to the shoulder and checked behind him for traffic. As he executed a U-turn, he said, "Where can we meet you?"

"Well, Mr. Shoemaker, you shouldn't be involved. This is police business. We'll notify you as soon as—"

Larry slammed his hand on the steering wheel. "Dammit! This is my sister, and I'm a retired cop—I know what I'm doing. I'm not going to sit and twiddle my thumbs."

The sheriff let out a sigh. "Fine. County Road X20 goes west about four miles north of Roswell. We're going to start there. I'm just coming into Roswell now."

"All right, we'll meet you there." Larry stomped a little on the gas.

Frannie switched off the phone. "X20, he said?"

"Yeah. Watch for it."

"Larry, why would one of their phones be moving and the other one not?"

"I don't know. Don't want to think about it. Maybe the guy found one of them and threw it out the window."

Traffic was light, and Larry made good time back to the intersection. An old rusty pickup careened out onto the highway just as Larry made his turn, barely missing them.

"Wow!" Frannie said. "He's in a hurry."

"Damn kids," Larry muttered. He was in no mood for teenaged antics. He pulled over to wait for the sheriff.

"The cell phone thing should be a good thing, right?"

"As long as the guy doesn't pitch them out somewhere," Larry said. "This could be a wild goose chase." He drummed his fingers on the steering wheel as he watched the road to the south. "I just can't figure why the guy would take off in this direction. Like the sheriff said, seems much more likely that he would head for Mexico or at least a state line. But we know from the gas station guy that they at least got to Roswell."

Frannie rested her forehead against the window, as she stared out at the desolate landscape. Why any of it, she thought.

In just a few minutes, the sheriff's SUV pulled up and Larry rolled down his window.

"Any more news?"

The sheriff shook his head. "I have the coordinates from the cell phone in my GPS so follow me."

As they bumped along, trying to stay back from the sheriff's dust, a little smile crept over Larry's mouth.

"What is it?" Frannie asked. It was the first smile she had seen on him all day.

"I was just thinking, if they came this way, how Mickey must have cringed at taking the Rocket down this road."

"You're not being very nice."

"When am I ever nice where Mickey is concerned?"

It was the kind of thing Larry would say when they were all together and having a great time. Under the circumstances, it brought tears to Frannie's eyes.

"Don't do it now, please."

He glanced at her. "Sorry. You're right."

Just then the sheriff slowed, pulled as far to the right as he could, and executed a tight U-turn. He lowered his window again.

"Just got a call that the cell phone is moving north on the highway we just left. Are you sure you didn't meet them?"

Larry shook his head. "Believe me, you can't miss that coach."

"Well, I'm heading that way." He took off in a swirl of dust. Larry managed to get turned around and followed him. When the sheriff got to the highway, he turned on his lights and siren and sped away, Larry on his tail. They passed several cars and RVs, a couple of semis, and a number of pickups, including a rusty rattletrap similar to the one that Larry and Frannie had met earlier. They continued north until they reached a rest area, and the sheriff signaled to pull in. Larry was out of the truck almost before it rolled to a stop.

"Now what?" he asked, as he ran to the sheriff. "Did you hear something else? Did they find them?"

Frannie had followed him, so that she could hear any news, too.

"They just told me they're behind us. We must have passed them."

Larry slapped the roof of the sheriff's vehicle. "We haven't passed them," he shouted. "We couldn't miss them."

Frannie put her hand on Larry's arm. "Larry, calm down. This isn't helping."

He shook her hand off and rubbed his hand over his crew cut, taking a deep breath. "Okay."

"We passed several RVs," the sheriff argued.

"And none of them were Mickey's. They must have pulled off on a side road."

"There aren't many."

"But it's the only explanation for us passing them," Larry said.

"All right, let's head back that way." The sheriff rolled up his window and started toward the highway entrance. Larry and Frannie ran to their truck, and soon they were back on the highway, headed south again. They met some of the vehicles they had passed on their way north, including the old pickup.

"Larry, that old truck we met at the side road..."

"That's not the same one."

"I know, but it reminded me. What if they ditched the Rocket and stole a truck? I mean, not Mickey and Jane Ann, but the Badger guy."

He thought about that. "You might be right. I've been assuming he wanted the coach to maybe live in, but I'm sure he's realized by now that it's pretty hard to hide. Call the sheriff and tell him about that truck. It was a Ford— probably twenty years old, beige with lots of rust."

113

The sheriff pulled off on the shoulder after Frannie's report, and Larry did likewise. He explained more completely their concerns about the truck. The sheriff took off his hat and scratched his head. He stood with his hands on his hips, staring off into the desert for a few moments.

"But it wasn't the truck that we passed going north?" he finally said.

"No, that just reminded us. The truck we saw must have turned off somewhere along this stretch."

"Could you tell who was driving?"

"Not really—a young man I think. It wasn't Mickey, but at least one other person was in there," Larry said.

"Okay. Let's keep going south and look for that truck. There were a few old farmsteads along the road. I'll put out a BOLO for it."

The search wasn't difficult since most of the roadside was desert, but each time they approached a house or buildings, the sheriff slowed down, and they scanned the area. There were old trucks a couple of places, but not the one they had seen. At the turnoff to County Road X20, they stopped again and waited for the sheriff to finish a call.

"They're still showing that cell phone in this area. I'm going to make one more pass, then I'm headed back to Roswell."

So back north they went, even slower this time. It seemed futile, considering how difficult it would be to hide anything in that landscape, until Frannie yelled, "Larry, pull over!"

He slowed down, edging onto the shoulder and was confused as his eyes swept the area. "What? There's nothing here." Endless brown dirt stretched as far as they could see, peppered with scrawny, dusty sage and bear grass, with a few clumps of stunted trees near a draw.

"I think that's Jane Ann's purse—there, near those trees by the gully. It's the one she bought when we were in Austin with Justine!" Frannie opened the door and slid out of the truck.

At first Larry's face showed relief, until the possible implications hit him. "Wait!"

The sheriff had stopped farther up the road and was backing up along the shoulder toward them. Frannie waited for Larry to come around the truck, and she pointed out the brightly colored striped fabric barely visible in one of the clumps of trees. She didn't know what it meant, but at least it was something.

Sheriff Parsons walked back to them, and she pointed out the purse. He led the way down toward the gully, pulling on gloves as he did so. He held some branches out of the way and picked up the purse by its wide strap. He set it on a nearby flat rock, crouched down, and gently opened the bag. Frannie scrutinized the rest of the area but saw nothing else. A relief of sorts.

He looked at Frannie. "Do you think you'll be able to tell if anything is missing?"

"Maybe—I know what she usually carried."

Kubrick first found a billfold, held it open, and looked questioningly at Frannie. There were no credit cards in the slots or cash in it. A couple of insurance cards were the only inhabitants.

"She always carried a small amount of cash and had at least two credit cards and a bank card," Frannie said.

The sheriff continued to search, finding a makeup bag, a package of tissues, a foldable shopping bag, a couple of postcards from Roswell, and, at the very bottom, a cell phone. Each item he extracted brought Frannie closer to tears.

"We'll get it checked for prints—especially the billfold. The purse won't show anything, being that rough fabric. I'm going to head back to Roswell and meet up with my deputies and other searchers there. We need a better plan of attack." He hesitated and looked at them directly. "I'm sorry to tell you that the other cell phone has either been turned off, gone dead or been broken. They've lost the signal."

Larry and Frannie put their arms around each other. Frannie had never seen Larry look so devastated.

Larry straightened up and cleared his throat. "Well." He looked at his watch. "We've got a few hours of light left. I'm going to drive down that X20 a way. What's out that way, anyway?"

"Not much—except where the supposed UFO crashed years ago. There's a few ranches and some crazies who are waiting for another landing. We don't mess with 'em as long as they don't cause trouble." He started to head for his car and turned back. "*Call* me if you see anything. *Don't* attempt to confront this guy on your own."

"I will," Larry said, but Frannie wasn't sure if he was sincere or not. Numerous times, they had confronted abductions and murders in campgrounds, and Larry was always adamant that Frannie stay out of it. Not that she listened much. But this was his sister, and it was hard telling what risks he would take.

THEY BOUNCED ALONG X20 and Frannie tried to peer in every crevice and behind rocks for any sign of the motorhome. One lane led off to the left to a small weathered ranch house a short distance from the road and a turn-around sat along the road on the right, but they spotted nothing suspicious.

The sky couldn't be any darker, and Frannie had never seen so many stars. The surreal shapes of the rocks picked out by the headlights made Frannie feel that she was the alien here. Larry tried a couple of lanes and dirt roads only leading to dead ends or abandoned farm houses. Finally, Larry pulled over in a flat area, and looked at her with despair.

"It's too dark," he said. "We can't drive this road without headlights, and with them, we certainly can't sneak up on anyone. We haven't eaten all day. I hate to quit, but I think we need to go back and start again in the morning. We'll stop at the police station and see if they've found anything."

Frannie's shoulders sagged, but she knew he was right. They headed back to the highway and turned toward Roswell. The silence in the truck was interrupted only by the thunk-thunk-thunk of the tires hitting the expansion joints in the pavement.

CHAPTER FIFTEEN
LATE THURSDAY AFTERNOON

Meanwhile, Badger had continued his protests all the way across the open area of the compound. He twisted to try to get out of Tobiah's grasp and lashed out with his foot in a side kick, but the bum was too fast for him. Then he spotted what he was sure was the motorhome, under cover, and to the side of the biggest building.

Maybe this wasn't all bad. He settled down and acted like he was beaten, watching for any opportunity of escape. Tobiah ushered him around the hidden coach to an area out behind the main building.

Flush with the ground was a wooden trap door about five-feet square. First Badger balked at the sight, and then stood quietly as Tobiah, still gripping Badger's arm, leaned down to pull the trapdoor open by means of a large ring. The hole in the ground was deep enough for a man to stand in and was lined with heavy wood planks.

Badger decided to try reasoning.

"Why don't you just let me go? I'm on the run—I ain't going to the cops about you guys."

Tobiah shook his head. "You're a murderer. Sit down on the edge."

"That ain't true. Those people are liars."

"I think I believe them. Sit."

Badger sat, hanging his head, and Tobiah kneeled behind him to undo his wrist restraints. Badger waited until he felt Tobiah's breath on his neck and threw his head back, hearing a satisfying CRACK. Of course, it made his own head hurt like hell, but Tobiah's groan of pain was a good deal, and Badger turned to see him sink to the ground. Badger jumped to his feet and dragged Tobiah to the edge of the pit, hesitated a moment, and searched his pockets. As he hoped, there were the keys to the motor home. He also found a gun in an ankle holster. With effort, he pushed Tobiah into the pit. He looked around, saw no one, and shut the trap door.

Badger could see an outcropping of rock a short distance to the northwest and made a beeline in that direction. The compound was built with all of the buildings facing the large open area and no windows in the back. The dusk would help cover his escape, too.

He reached the rocks and hid where he could just look over the top of a big boulder. No sign of anyone. He took stock of his situation. Actually he was right back where he had been in the hills above the campground. Free, but absolutely no supplies with which to strike out across the desert. He knew he was somewhere northwest of Roswell, but that was about it.

He'd only been in New Mexico a short time, when that dirt bag he met in a bar talked him into a "sure thing" heist of a convenience store. How were they to know the clerk would have a gun hidden under the counter? Badger fired in self-defense, that's all it was. But the stupid court didn't see it that way.

If he had been in northern Wisconsin, surviving would be no problemo. There was plenty of water and good hiding places. There were enough occasional summer cabins that could be broken into for supplies. Escape would be a snap for a guy like him.

But here? He looked around at the desolate landscape. DeWayne was the one who always wanted to go to "The Land of Enchantment," he called it. Some enchantment. More like cursed. Badger didn't know why anyone would want to live here.

So. That was all poop down the toilet, as his foster father would have said. Right now he had to figure out how he was going to get out of here. When he saw where the motorhome was hidden, he had thought he could use it to get out. But, he would have to wait until full dark to try for that, and by that time he hoped they would give up looking for him.

He pulled back in the rocks to wait.

"WELL, NOW WHAT?" Mickey said, as he struggled with his ropes.

"I don't have any ideas," Jane Ann said.

"I know. I just meant I wonder what's next. You know, they don't seem very inclined to just let us go, but they don't seem violent either."

Jane Ann cocked her head. "Mick—did you forget already that she ushered us up here with a gun?"

"She hasn't used it on us yet," Mickey said.

"No, just on our motorhome."

"I know." Mickey hung his head.

"You said you think your phone is in your pocket?"

""Yeah, but...Wait! Can you scoot your chair this way and maybe get it? It's in my left pocket."

"I'll try." Jane Ann tried moving forward on the rough wood floor, but got her feet tangled in the rungs and nearly pitched forward. Instead she worked on sliding sideways towards Mickey. Several times, the chair leg caught in gaps between the boards, and she had to jerk the chair out and over the gap.

She stopped to rest and looked at her husband. "This is a classic case of 'you could meet me halfway.'"

Mickey looked embarrassed—not a common expression for him. "Oh! I'm sorry. I will." And he began sliding his chair toward her. They took turns hopping and scooting their chairs toward each other to keep the noise level down.

Finally, they were near enough to touch and Jane Ann turned her chair enough to reach Mickey's pocket. With her hands tied behind the chair, she couldn't see what she was doing and had to rely on Mickey's direction.

"There. No, up an inch or two. Feel the edge? You're almost there."

Jane Ann managed to get two fingers into the pocket. She leaned her chair back to get closer. She grasped the edge of the phone between her first and second fingers and carefully pulled it up.

"I understand now the importance of opposable thumbs," she said, as she worked to get it out of the pocket. "How are we going to dial—"

She was interrupted by a noise at the door, and the phone slipped out of her fingers, skidding across the floor. It stopped right in front of the door as it swung open and Maranatha stepped in. The shotgun was still slung under her arm.

She looked at the phone and then at them. Jane Ann felt like she had been caught being naughty by spinning a ruler on her pencil in third grade. She prepared for a scolding.

Maranatha glanced at the phone at her feet again, raised one foot, and stomped it with the heel of her cowboy boot. The screen shattered and splinters flew across the floor.

Mickey squirmed in his chair and shouted, "What did you do that for?"

"Obviously, you can't be trusted," Maranatha said. She opened the door and called, "Eli! Come here!"

When the young man entered, he looked with surprise at the two prisoners so close together.

"We're going to move them to the main house. Untie them from the chairs but tie their hands back up." She kept the shotgun pointed at them.

Eli carried out her orders without a word. Jane Ann took advantage of the short reprieve to stretch and rub her chafed wrists. Soon enough, he had retied the rope, but it didn't seem quite as tight. Once he was done, Maranatha gestured with her gun for Eli to lead Mickey and Jane Ann out ahead of her. Jane Ann wondered if the woman put her gun down to eat supper.

As they stumbled out the door into the brighter light — a brilliant crimson and gold New Mexico sunset colored the western sky — Jane Ann also wondered what Larry and Frannie were doing, knowing how frantic they must be. And where the police were searching for them. Did her attempt to dial Larry's number go through? As she slowed to take in the surrounding landscape, Eli gave her a shove to keep her moving.

"Hey!" Mickey said. "That isn't necessary!"

"Shut up," Maranatha said, and he received a prod in the ribs for emphasis.

A girl of about seven or eight stood watching their approach.

"Who are them, Miss Maranatha?"

"Busybodies," Maranatha said, as they reached the building with the planet carved above the door.

"Wait!" Mickey stopped and turned to Eli. "Where's our camper?"

Maranatha had turned to answer a question from another resident, so Eli just nodded his head toward the side of the building. Camouflage fabric and pine branches covered a large object — the Red Rocket. Mickey grinned and winked at the young man. Eli ducked his head to hide his little smile from Maranatha as she turned back to open the door.

It opened into a great room, lined with long tables and bracketed at each end with immense stone fireplaces. A few people had gathered around each fireplace, while others set the tables for supper.

Maranatha led her prisoners toward the long side of the room opposite the door, and it was then that Jane Ann noticed the apparatuses standing like sentinels in the middle of the back wall. There were three pillories of the type used in colonial times to imprison people — usually for public ridicule. Perhaps they were just historical pieces — reminders of days gone by?

Eli produced a set of ancient keys on a ring and unlocked two of the pillories. Jane Ann looked at Mickey. Not just historical artifacts then. They were ushered around behind the frames, and, after their hands were untied, they were directed to put their heads and hands in the appropriate slots. The devices had no foot holes, as stocks did. They had to stand, but bent at an awkward and painful angle that was sure to put them both in traction if they ever made it out of here.

Conversation died as everyone in the room turned to stare at them. Table setting stopped for a few moments, as the workers took in the scene. The little girl who had questioned Maranatha peeked from behind an older woman, and then edged toward them.

"What did you do?" she asked, when she got close enough.

"Nothing, sweetie," Mickey said. "We were just trying to live our lives."

"Jerusha!" called the older woman in a sharp voice. "Come here!"

Jerusha started to turn, but said, "Is that hard?"

"It is today," Mickey said.

Jerusha shrugged and returned to the woman, perhaps her grandmother. Like a slow motion carousel that had been momentarily suspended in time, people continued their meal preparations, mostly ignoring their reluctant guests.

CHAPTER SIXTEEN

THURSDAY EVENING

LARRY PARKED NEAR the Chavez County Courthouse where the sheriff's department was located, and they both got out. Inside, at the desk, Larry explained their presence, and that they were looking for Sheriff Parsons. The sheriff stepped out of an office behind the desk and motioned them in. Frannie almost didn't recognize him without his Stetson.

"I assume you didn't find anything, or I would have heard from you?" It was a statement but posed as a question.

"Nothing," Larry said.

The sheriff motioned them to empty chairs and introduced them to Deputy Luisa McClarty and Deputy Sam Jones. Ironically, considering their names, Luisa was tall with light brown hair and freckles, and Jones appeared very Hispanic.

"We just got fingerprint results on that purse. Couple of young men from up the road a piece—not Baxter Bagley. We think they found that purse somewhere, and we need to find out where. A possession of stolen goods charge should go a long way in getting that information.

Jones and McClarty here are about to go out and pick them up, hopefully."

Larry leaned forward in his chair. "You've located them?"

"We know where they live," the sheriff said.

"But they may not be there," Larry said.

"We have a BOLO out, too." Sheriff Parsons shuffled some papers on his desk. "You should probably go back to the campground, get some rest, and we'll call as soon as we have something."

Frannie expected a protest, but Larry surprised her.

"Okay. I'll leave you to do your job. But, seriously, I do want to know as soon as you bring them in." He stood up. "Thank you, Sheriff." He nodded to the two deputies, and Frannie followed him out.

THEY DIDN'T SPEAK until they were back in the truck.

"I didn't expect you to go along with the sheriff," Frannie said. "Or was that a smokescreen?"

Larry crossed his arms on the steering wheel and rested his head a moment, then sat up and turned to her.

"I don't know what to do. But I don't know the country, and I'm sure those deputies do. I'll give them a chance. You haven't heard from Mom again, have you?"

"No. So what now?"

He started the truck. "Let's pick up some carryout somewhere, go back to the camper, and wait for the sheriff's call. Maybe we can get a little rest."

They picked up fried rice and beef and broccoli stir-fry at a Chinese place on the highway and headed south to the campground.

BACK IN THEIR CAMPER, Frannie got out plates and flatware, mainly because she felt they needed some kind of normalcy.

Larry pushed his food around his plate, and then looked up at her across the dinette.

"If they're okay, I'll never pick on Mickey again."

"Of course you will." Frannie smiled—weak but a smile. "Mickey will think you don't like him if you quit picking on him."

Larry shrugged and looked around the camper. "Maybe we should sell this thing and just stay home."

"I know you're hurting, and you think there's something you should have done, but this isn't your fault."

"If only I had locked that compartment."

"You don't know that that would have prevented this. Or him taking someone else—which would have been easier on us, granted, but some other family would have to deal with it."

"Usually, *I'm* the one telling *you* that." He smiled.

She took his hand. "I know. That's why our marriage has survived this long without one of us killing the other. We balance each other out."

He dug into his plate. "Let's finish and take a walk around the campground. I feel like I've been in a box all day."

"You have."

His phone rang, and he snatched it up without looking at the screen. "Hullo?" After listening a few seconds, he said to Frannie, "Bob," and turned back to the phone. "It was on the news?" He then brought his brother up to date on the events since the morning. "So the sheriff is going to try and find these hoodlums that had her purse. Maybe we can get a fix on where they got it." He rubbed his forehead. "I understand, but there's nothing you can do. Mom called this morning to tell Jane Ann that her friend Betsy is in town--we're trying to stall her. Have you heard from her?' A pause. "If you do, don't say anything. She'll have a heart attack." They spoke a few minutes more, and Larry assured Bob that he would call as soon as he knew anything.

Larry punched off his phone and laid it on the table. "He offered to come over," he said to Frannie, "But of course, there's nothing he can do, and he's about eight hours away."

Frannie nodded. "The only thing worse than being here and helpless would be being faraway and helpless. Does Elaine know?"

"He's going to call her. It won't be pretty." Elaine was known in the family as something of a drama queen.

"In this instance, I wouldn't blame her," Frannie said.

They ate their small helpings, took care of the leftovers, and put their jackets back on. Even though they were going to be nearby, Larry locked the camper, and they started out around the loop.

The air was crisp and felt refreshing after the closed cab in the pickup all day. As they neared Palmer Pierce's motorhome, they noticed that the tent and Mark Cullen's campsite had been cleared. Such a young man to have his life ended so suddenly. Frannie wondered if he had any family.

Palmer was outside, folding lawn chairs and storing them in one of the compartments. He looked up and waved, concern on his face over what the results of their day had been.

"Your friends—?"

"Haven't found them yet, but they have some leads that sound promising," Larry said. Frannie thought that he would have made a good media representative for the police. Except that the Perfection Falls Police didn't have much call to deal with the media.

Palmer put down the lawn chair and walked over to them. "I'm so sorry. Would you like to come in and have a beer? A little chilly out here tonight."

"Oh, no," Larry said. "Looks like you're packing up."

"I need a break." Palmer laughed. "Like I've been working hard. Come in and meet my wife and tell us about your day."

Larry looked at Frannie, and she nodded. "Well, just for a few minutes. Are you taking off tomorrow?"

Palmer opened the door for them. "Yup. Headed to Palo Duro Canyon in Texas. Ever been there?"

"Not yet," Frannie said. "We've heard it's beautiful."

"Peg!" Palmer called toward the back of the coach. "Company!"

The woman who emerged from the bedroom was nearly as tall as Palmer and a striking blonde. She too was extremely tan, but as she got closer, Frannie could see the weathering in her face. Her smile, however, was warm and welcoming.

"These are the people I told you about—the one's whose friends disappeared this morning."

Frannie and Larry introduced themselves.

"I am so sorry," Peg Pierce said, holding out her hand. "Please have a seat." They sat, and Frannie's gaze took in the sumptuous coach.

"Thank you," Larry said. "Actually, Jane Ann and her husband are my sister and brother-in-law."

"That's even worse," Peg said, stuffing a wisp of hair into her sleek ponytail. "Have you heard anything?"

Palmer handed them each a beer as Larry recounted their frustrations of the day. He checked his phone twice during the story. "Oh, oh," he said after the first time.

"What?" Frannie said, alarmed, as she gripped his arm.

He broke into a sheepish grin. "Mom. She apparently called again a little while ago."

"She must be very worried," Peg said.

They watched in silence as the photo of Mickey and Jane Ann in front of the Red Rocket shared the screen with a mug shot of Baxter Bagley.

When the report finished, Larry said, "I'm going to try to catch some sleep here in my chair."

"I'll take the couch," Frannie said and went into the bedroom to grab a pillow and a couple of blankets. She laid down fully dressed, and Larry shut off the lights except the dim stove light. They both had their phones at hand.

Frannie closed her eyes and tried to shut off her worries. She thought about the great times they had spent in beautiful places, hiking, laughing around the fire, or swooning over delicious meals. She concentrated on the wonder of some of those places. Most of those times had been spent with the Ferraros. She focused on the joys of spending time with her grandchildren, but then remembered how much Mickey and Jane Ann enjoyed them as well. It was no use.

So she tried to think of anything else they could be doing. In an unfamiliar area, with no friends or family around, there wasn't much. She squirmed on the couch trying to get comfortable, and she could hear Larry doing the same in the recliner. Apparently, they both were avoiding the bed because they didn't want to get too comfortable and miss a call.

But she must have dozed off because the shrill screech of Larry's phone jolted her awake. The phone clattered to the floor as he reached for it and missed. He swore and managed to find it.

"Hello? Yes—okay. Thanks."

Frannie had switched on the light and looked at him questioningly.

"They caught those kids, and they have finally admitted they took the purse from the motorhome. They are going to lead the sheriff to it, and he's leaving in about twenty minutes. We can just make it."

The clock said 3:00.

Chapter Seventeen
Thursday Evening

BECAUSE THE PILLORY confined their heads with their necks bent, it was difficult to watch what was happening in the large hall. From time to time, they craned their necks sideways enough to get a glimpse, but Jane Ann's neck was beginning to feel chafed as well as shot through with pain.

After the tables were all set, steaming bowls were brought out and placed in the middle. Jane Ann couldn't tell what was in them, but there was a strong smell of cabbage. Shuffling footsteps and the scraping of benches heralded the arrival of the diners. Jane Ann took a look as it quieted — all ages appeared to be represented and there was very little talking. She caught Mickey's eye as she turned, and again worried about his health. His face appeared almost gray.

"This isn't happening, right?" he croaked.

"Quiet!" came a harsh voice behind them.

Jane Ann didn't realize anyone was back there and whipped her head up, cracking the back of her skull on the top part of the pillory. She moaned and Mickey tried to see who their watcher was, but, of course, with no success.

"Are we going to get anything to eat or drink?" he asked the disembodied voice.

"Quiet!" the voice said again.

Mickey had no comeback, reaffirming Jane Ann's concern about his well-being. She tried to reach his left hand with her right but couldn't.

As people finished their meal, individuals at each table collected the dishes and flatware. Conversation was still very subdued. Two young men appeared in front of them with bowls and cups with straws. They kneeled in front of Mickey and Jane Ann like supplicants. The sight was so ludicrous, Jane Ann almost laughed out loud.

One of them frowned and started spooning a gray mix of some kind of meal and cabbage in Jane Ann's mouth, while the other man did the same to Mickey. They scooped spoonfuls as if they were feeding a furnace, and when Mickey and Jane Ann began choking and coughing the stuff back out, the men held the cups up and stuck the straws in their mouths. Jane Ann took a drink of the tepid water, wanted to spit it out, but knew she was already dehydrated and swallowed.

The man feeding Jane Ann went back to the sticky bowl, but she shook her head. "Just water, please." Mickey did the same. When they had drunk their fill, the men tried to go back to the food, but again their prisoners refused.

"You have to eat this. We can't throw food out," the one feeding Jane Ann said. He glanced back over his shoulder with a look of concern. Jane Ann reluctantly opened her mouth. Just then there was a commotion at the door. Jane Ann managed to look up enough to see a man, followed by Eli, burst in and call for Maranatha.

She had been standing at one end of the room talking to another woman, when she heard her name. She picked up her shotgun, which was leaning against a chair, and strode over to the door. Eli and the other man talked excitedly with lots of gestures, and all three went back out the door.

The two men feeding Mickey and Jane Ann set the bowls on the floor, and followed the others. No sooner were they out the door, than a red-haired man with a beard jumped up on a little platform at one end of the room.

"Listen! Listen! Maranatha has it wrong!" he yelled.

The people still in the room turned toward him, looks of shock on their faces.

"When the aliens get here, it won't be to save us! They are nothing more than demons, disguised as aliens! They are fallen angels, I tell you! We can't go with them!"

The crowd erupted.

"What? No!"

"Blaspheme!"

"Get him!"

Several nearby charged the platform and wrestled the man to the ground. Maranatha and the men came back in at that point. Tobiah followed them, hanging his head and only giving quick sideways glances at the crowd. Maranatha stalked to the little stage.

"What's going on here?" she demanded, her shotgun tucked under her arm.

"He blasphemed!" a woman shouted, pointing, and leaned over to whisper in Maranatha's ear, as if the whole room hadn't heard what had been said.

Maranatha drew to her full height and pointed at two of the men. "You, and you — take him to the snake pit!"

"But what about the Stranger?" one of the men asked.

"He's gone!" With that Maranatha marched over to the pillory.

"Where did your friend go?" she asked Jane Ann and Mickey.

Mickey's voice came out in a croak. "We told you. He's not our friend. He kidnapped us."

Jane Ann decided to take a chance. "Ma'am? Could you please let us go to the bathroom?"

Maranatha looked like she was going to turn them down, and then thought about the consequences. Instead she turned and called," Selah! Tobiah!"

When they reached Maranatha, she said "Take them to the bathrooms. Don't take your eyes off of them. See if you can handle this, Tobiah."

Behind them, someone — the owner of the voice apparently — unlocked the padlocks and raised the top of the pillories. Selah helped Jane Ann to stand and gave her a minute to get her bearings.

"Are you dizzy?"

"A little," Jane Ann said. She shook her hands. "I think my hands went to sleep."

"I know," Selah said, and the conviction in her voice told Jane Ann that she knew from experience. What kind of place was this anyway? she thought again.

Mickey, too, looked a little disoriented, as Selah and Tobiah tied their wrists again. Selah led Jane Ann and Tobiah pushed Mickey ahead of him toward the door. The crowd parted and backed up like they were afraid of contamination. Outside the building, they were led in opposite directions. Selah took Jane Ann to the east end of the compound. A row of wooden outhouses stood like sentinels. Selah knocked on the door of one, and when she received no answer, untied Jane Ann's wrists and opened the door.

Jane Ann didn't think Selah was armed, and she seemed so fragile that Jane Ann was sure she could take her, or at least knock her down. But she wouldn't leave without Mickey, and even if she could rescue him, it would be crazy to strike out from here without supplies or knowing where they were. Apparently that's what Badger had done, but that just proved the point — crazy.

When she came out of the outhouse, she said to Selah, "Is there some place I can wash my hands?"

Selah pointed to a large covered barrel at the end of the row of outhouses. Jane Ann stepped over to the barrel and removed the lid. The stagnant odor wafted up and hit her in the face, but she tried to block it out and dipped her hands in.

Selah said, "There's soap there on the side." A bar of handmade soap hung by a string. Jane Ann used it, thankful for small favors, and wondered what her college nursing instructors would think of this hand-washing facility. Actually, she didn't wonder at all; she knew.

Selah retied her hands, and they walked back toward the main building.

"Where do you get your water?" Jane Ann asked for the sake of conversation.

"We have a well. But we conserve it very carefully. You have to take care of the earth."

"You're right; we do."

"Where are you from?" Selah asked.

Jane Ann was surprised, as this was the first indication of interest that Selah had shown in them. "We're from Iowa."

"Is that where they grow potatoes?"

Jane Ann laughed. "No, that's Idaho. We grow corn."

"I've never been out of New Mexico," Selah said. "Do you have children?"

"Two daughters. They're both grown. One is in college in Iowa, and the other is married and lives in Texas. She is expecting a baby girl, so I will be a grandmother soon, too." She thought, nobody wants to kill a grandmother, right?

"Ohhhh." Selah almost swooned, and Jane Ann thought it was at the mention of a baby, but then Selah said, "College" in a dreamy voice.

They had reached the main building, and Mickey and Tobiah were already back. Jane Ann managed to squeeze Mickey's hand, and he winked at her. Tobiah and Selah seemed uncertain what to do with them. For a moment Jane Ann hoped maybe Maranatha would relent on their treatment, but she turned around, spotted them, and said "Get them back in the pillory. We don't want any more escapes."

By now, the large room was mostly empty. When they were first put in the pillories, it took a while before Jane Ann became really uncomfortable. Now the aches and pains returned almost instantly.

Maranatha was at the other end of the hall talking with Tobiah, and no one had come to guard them. Jane Ann turned her head toward Mickey.

"Did you learn anything from Tobiah on your bathroom trip?"

"Just that Badger escaped by knocking Tobiah out and pushing him in the snake pit, and that Maranatha doesn't know yet what she's going to do with us. She seems convinced that we're spies sent in by the government," Mickey said.

"Seems ridiculous, but I guess that would be a clever cover," Jane Ann admitted.

"These people are really paranoid. And paranoid people are scary."

Tobiah went to a closet and brought out a folding cot.

Mickey brightened. "Maybe they're going to let us lay down to sleep?"

Not to be. Tobiah set the cot up about twenty feet away from them. He then returned to the closet for a blanket and a pillow. After arranging them on the cot, he laid down. Maranatha extinguished all of the lanterns but one and left.

Mickey sighed. "And maybe not. Tobiah? Tobiah!"

The young man rolled over and opened one eye at them.

"Yes?"

"We can't stay in these things all night. We're not young any more. We'll be crippled for life."

If they still *had* a life, Jane Ann thought.

"Well, I can't let you just roam around," Tobiah said, and started to turn back away from them.

"Wait!" Mickey said. "What about letting one of us lay down at a time? Neither of us is going to run away and leave the other one here." He glanced at Jane Ann for reassurance, and she almost laughed at the tiny glimmer of doubt in his eyes.

"No, we're not," she said firmly.

Tobiah shook his head. "I can't do that. I'll be in trouble."

Jane Ann took up the cause. "You'll be in bigger trouble if one or both of us dies. They are looking for us,

and they *will* eventually find us. My brother is a cop."
Only fudging the truth a little, she thought. "If we're
dead, *someone* will be charged with murder." She left the
thought hanging..

He was considering it, they could tell. He shook his
head again, but he wasn't so certain this time. "I don't
know..."

"Please." Jane Ann pushed. "Mickey's health already
is bad."

Tobiah got up and pushed back his hair. He sat on the
edge of the cot for a moment, leaning on his arms with
his head hanging down. Finally he looked up. "One of
you at a time, and you have to lay on the floor right here
by the cot. I'll tie your wrist to mine."

"Oh, thank you," Jane Ann said. "Anything to lay
down for a little bit."

"You go first," Mickey said.

"Are you sure?"

"Yeah, gives me something to look forward to." He
grinned.

"You're hopeless," she said.

Tobiah went behind them to get the key for the
pillory and unlocked Jane Ann's side. He led her by the
arm over to the cot and motioned her down on the floor.
Not much of a talker, Jane Ann thought. Once she lay
down, he tied his right wrist to her left.

"Thank you," she said again.

In spite of the hard rough floor, she took a deep
breath and stretched every muscle she could.

"What are you doing?" Jane Ann could detect a note of panic in Tobiah's voice.

"Just trying to stretch a little. I got pretty stiff in that thing."

"All right. Lay still now."

Mickey fortunately kept quiet.

JANE ANN SLEPT deep and heavy, but woke with a start after a couple of hours. She raised her arm to look at her watch, and in doing so woke Tobiah.

"What?" He sat up and looked around, trying to get his bearings.

"Can we trade places now? I know Mickey needs to lay down," Jane Ann said.

"You are sure a lot of trouble," Tobiah said. He got up and helped Jane Ann to her feet. Once he had her untied and back in the pillory, he opened Mickey's side, put the key in his pocket, and led him over to the floor by the cot.

Jane Ann was still groggy and fought nodding off, although she was sure that if her head dropped, the bottom edge of the neck hole would cut off her windpipe and wake her immediately. She hoped.

Tobiah was soon snoring. Jane Ann heard very soft rustling coming from Mickey.

"What are you doing?" she whispered.

"Shhh," was the only response.

About fifteen minutes passed, and Mickey was standing in front of Jane Ann.

"I got my wrist untied. He didn't do a very good job of it," he said quietly. "I don't want to try to get the key for the pillory out of his pocket, until I know we can get out of here. I'm going to go see if they left the keys in the motorhome."

"Okay," she said. "My hero." She could just barely make out his grin in the low light.

He tiptoed to the door and opened it just far enough to slip through. Jane Ann was surprised that Maranatha hadn't locked them in.

The wait seemed interminable. She couldn't hear a sound. Until a motor started and the Red Rocket pulled away. Very fast.

BADGER THOUGHT ABOUT how much time he had spent in the last couple of days waiting in the rocks. It better be worth it. Lights went out early in the compound. But he waited for what he thought were a couple of hours before making his move.

By the time he reached the motorhome, a thin moon was rising. He carefully pulled the camouflage and branches off toward the back of the coach. When he had it clear, he pulled the keys out of his pocket, and climbed into the driver's seat. He looked around at the dash, turned the key, and barreled off into the night.

LARRY AND FRANNIE arrived at the sheriff's office just inside the twenty minutes. Sheriff Parsons was waiting by his cruiser, and Frannie could see two sullen teenagers in the back seat.

Larry pulled up and rolled down his window and the sheriff walked over.

"Their story is that that motorhome was parked along X20 in an open spot. One of the tires was shot up, and the coach was open, so they just grabbed the purse. They took off when they heard someone coming."

"The tire was shot up?" Larry said.

The sheriff shrugged. "That's what they said. McClarty and Jones are going to follow me; you follow them, okay?"

Larry nodded, thinking about the implications.

COUNTY ROAD X20 hadn't improved in the hours since Frannie and Larry had been that way earlier. Frannie hung on as they bounced along trying to keep up. A few miles down the road, the sheriff slowed and the other vehicles followed suit. As they approached the pullout, headlights reflected off the rocks opposite. A large white and red vehicle careened out in front of the sheriff, forcing him off the road.

The sight of the Red Rocket shooting past them headed for the highway brought Frannie's heart into her throat. Larry screeched to a halt behind the deputies and jumped out of his truck leaving the door ajar. He ran up to the sheriff, nearly getting hit by the deputies' car as they executed a sharp U-turn in the narrow road.

Sheriff Parsons lowered his window.

"That's them!" Larry shouted, before Parsons could say anything.

"I know — sent McClarty and Jones after them. I'll get turned around and follow." He didn't wait for Larry's response but edged up to the pullout, turned, and was soon back on the road. Larry raced back to the truck and brought up the rear.

Larry leaned forward over the steering wheel, willing the convoy to go faster.

"Could you see who was driving?" he asked Frannie.

"Just a glimpse in our headlights — I'm sure it wasn't Mickey. Must be Badger. What if he dumped them somewhere? Something isn't right. If a tire was ruined, I'm sure Mickey couldn't change it. He always calls a roadside service."

Frannie thought about that. "Maybe someone lives back there — it looked like a lane went back through the rocks when we went by there yesterday. I remember thinking it's a good thing they don't get snow like we do in Iowa, or it would be drifted shut all winter."

147

"What are you saying?"

"I don't really know. What time did we meet that pickup?"

"Must have been around 2:00? I figured we had a couple of hours of light left after we found her purse."

Frannie said, "So about twelve hours ago. The Rocket wasn't there when we drove down that road later, so where was it? Why is Badger just now trying to get out of here? What's he been doing since then?"

"Sleeping?" Larry said. He shook his head. "Sorry — probably not. You're wondering what's down that lane, right?"

"I guess. I didn't see anyone in the passenger seat when they went by."

Larry pulled over on the shoulder. "He could have them tied up in the back." The possibility of worse remained unspoken. He pulled back on the road. "I understand what you're saying, but I still think our best bet is to find out who's in that motorhome and go from there. Despite Mickey's name for his coach, the Rocket isn't going to outrun any squad cars."

They reached the highway and once again turned north. Although they had lost sight of the sheriff's cars, it didn't seem likely that Badger would elect to go back to Roswell. Larry bumped the speed of the truck up, and about five miles later, they spotted flashing lights at the side of the road, and in their glow, the Red Rocket.

Larry pulled onto the shoulder behind the sheriff's car. The deputies had cut the Rocket off by pulling ahead of them. Frannie started to open the door, but Larry reached over and put his hand on her shoulder.

"Wait a minute. Parsons is crouched between his car and the Rocket. He has his gun out."

Frannie nodded and peered into the ditch area, struggling to distinguish the players in the alternating darkness and flashing lights.

"I can see somebody...I think Badger's out by the side of the coach, and it looks like he has Mickey," she said. "What can we do?"

"They need a distraction. I'm sure that McClarty and Jones are trying to move in from the other direction." Larry looked around the cab and peered over into the back seat. "Mickey's UFO!"

"What are you talking about?" Frannie asked.

Larry reached over and pulled a shopping bag out of the footwell. "This. Mickey left it here so he wouldn't be tempted to get it out and play with it. He said it has lights and a remote control." He pulled a box out of the sack and tore it open.

Plastic encased the device along with batteries and the remote. He handed Frannie the instructions while he tried frantically to remove the packaging.

"These damn things—we don't have scissors in here, do we?"

"No. How about a nail clippers?" She pulled one out of her purse.

He took it and poked and clipped until the plastic surrendered. A remote fell in his lap that reminded Frannie of the transistor radios of her youth.

Frannie pored over the instructions. "You only need one of the batteries. There's a spare."

Larry found the compartment and inserted the battery. He looked toward the sheriff's car and could see Parsons still in place through the windows. He flicked a switch on the remote and the thing sprang to life. He turned it back off and climbed out of the truck, careful not to bump the fragile device.

"I'm coming too," Frannie said. "Don't close the door, because I'd better not get out this side. I'll bring the controller."

Easier said than done. She felt like she was trying out for the Olympic gymnastics team, but finally managed to clamber over the console and under the wheel to get out.

Larry was already talking to the sheriff in low whispers. Frannie caught up to him.

"Is my sister in there?" Larry was saying.

"We don't know—he has your brother-in-law outside by the door, and somewhere he's gotten a gun. Does your brother-in-law own one?"

"Absolutely not. He hates them. He held up the drone. "This was in my truck—Mickey bought it the other day. It has a camera. Can we use it to distract him, and, at the same time, see what's going on?"

Parsons looked at him like he was nuts. "I just said, he has a gun."

Larry wasn't swayed. "He's less likely to shoot Mickey if something sails over his head, than if you guys play swat team and surround him."

"McClarty and Jones won't know what you're doing."

"I'll go tell them," Frannie whispered. "But we need a signal. Larry can monitor when Badger gets distracted and then you guys could move in?"

"Okay, it might work," the sheriff said. "As well as anything, I guess. But he'll hear a whistle or anything like that."

"I'll stay down there but behind the coach. When you raise your hand, Larry, I'll tell them to go," Frannie said. And off she went. As she trotted along the coach, she wanted to yell, "Jane Ann, are you in there?"

The two deputies were crouched at the front of the coach. McClarty was talking in a low, reasonable tone to Badger, who was around the corner on the side of the coach. Frannie motioned to Jones to join her on the opposite side.

She explained what Larry planned to do and told him to watch for her signal. He looked skeptical but nodded.

Larry had moved to the corner where he could see her and launched the drone. He was concentrating on the controller.

The rumble of running motors masked the voices from the other side of the coach. The flashing lights of the drone created almost a Northern Lights effect in the sky over the motorhome. But Frannie reminded herself to watch Larry as he focused on the controller screen. Finally he looked up and signaled Go! to her. She ducked around the corner of the coach and said "*Go!*" to Deputy Jones. He pushed McClarty ahead of him as he growled, "Get him!"

A shot pierced the engine sounds and Frannie's stomach turned. Mickey! By the time Frannie had rounded the corner, McClarty had Badger on the ground, but Mickey was standing, clutching his arm, blood trickling between his fingers. Jones helped Mickey remove his windbreaker so he could examine the wound.

Sheriff Parsons jerked Badger to his feet and handcuffed him, while Larry and Frannie descended on Mickey.

"Did you get shot?" Frannie asked, but Larry cut right to the chase.

"Is Jane Ann inside?"

Mickey shook his head, and his eyes teared up. Frannie didn't want to know what that meant; she wanted to cover her ears.

"She's still back at that loony farm."

Larry grabbed his shoulder — fortunately not the one that had been hit. "What loony farm? Where?"

"Larry, take it easy," Frannie said, pulling him back. Her heart lifted a little at Mickey's words.

"I know. I know." Larry ran his hand over his crew cut. "Sorry, buddy."

Mickey turned to the sheriff, who had just turned Badger over to McClarty. "We need to get back there."

"You need to go to the hospital," the sheriff said. "Where is this place? Can you tell us?"

"I don't need a hospital until we rescue my wife. There's a first aid kit in the coach. I think the bullet just grazed me."

Sheriff Parsons looked exasperated. He took off his hat and slapped it against his leg. "McClarty!" he barked. "You have EMT training, dontcha?"

"Yessir."

"Have Jones take Bagley to town and you get back here."

"Where's the first aid kit, Mickey?" Frannie asked.

Mickey appeared to be getting dizzy. "Under the driver's seat."

"Mr. Ferraro, you need to at least sit down," Deputy McClarty said. She motioned toward the door of the coach. "Can we go inside? I'll look at your arm while you tell us what happened." Frannie returned from the driver's side with the kit and followed the deputy and Mickey into the side door. The sheriff and Larry brought up the rear.

McClarty sat Mickey down on the couch and pushed up his shirtsleeve. The others tried to find places to stand out of the way.

"What's the 'loony farm,' Mickey?" Larry said. "Where is it?"

Mickey leaned his head back on the couch. "Back...toward Roswell...a gravel road. X20, I think." He took a deep breath and winced as McClarty cleaned his wound. "About five or six miles in, there's a pullout on the right...but there's a lane that goes back...hard to see. You gotta go get her, Larry. Those people are nuts." He wiped his eyes.

The sheriff nodded as Mickey described the location. "All right, you and McClarty ride with me. I think we know where you mean. We'll lock this rig up and get it later. You can guide me." He looked at Larry. "Are you following?"

"Absolutely," Larry said. "Mickey, why is Jane Ann back there?"

"These crazies were holding us all prisoner. She shot a tire out on the Rocket." He paused and shook his head. "Somehow Badger got away. In the night I got loose and went to see if the keys were in the Rocket. If they were, I was going to unlock Jane Ann, and we would get away. But while I was searching for the keys, Badger got in and drove away. He didn't even know I was in here until we stopped."

"Unlock Jane Ann? What do you mean...?"

The sheriff held up his hand. "Gotta get going. McClarty, you got that arm bandaged?"

"Yessir." The deputy helped Mickey stand and out the door. Soon they were back on the deserted road. Larry followed the sheriff's U-turn and they sped through the night.

CHAPTER NINETEEN
THURSDAY NIGHT

JANE ANN WAS DUMFOUNDED. She had heard the unmistakable sound of the Rocket driving off, but she couldn't believe it. No way Mickey would leave her here. Did Maranatha catch him and decide to move the vehicle somewhere else? But wouldn't she have returned Mickey to the pillory first?

Jane Ann wasn't the only one who was startled. Tobiah jerked upright and looked at the rope dangling from his wrist. As realization dawned, he jumped up.

"Where'd he go?" he demanded of Jane Ann.

"I don't know," she answered, her voice breaking.

"Now you've done it! Maranatha will never let you live after this!" The way his voice quavered, Jane Ann suspected he was concerned about his own neck as well. He turned and headed for the door just as it burst open. Maranatha, her hair wild and wearing a barn coat over men's pajamas stood swinging a lantern in one hand and brandishing her shotgun in the other. The frenzied look in her eyes reminded Jane Ann of the pictures in history books of the abolitionist, John Brown.

"What is going on? Where did that RV go?"

Tobiah bent at the waist like a supplicant. He was shaking.

"I'm sorry...I don't know what..."

She looked over at Jane Ann and took in the empty pillory. "Where's the other prisoner?" She was screeching now.

Jane Ann took a deep breath and spoke loudly. "I don't know what happened, but he wouldn't have gone voluntarily and left me here."

Maranatha sauntered toward her with a smirk on her face. "Well, obviously he did."

"No, I know he didn't. Someone else drove off with him." She wanted to shake her head and felt cheated that even that simple pleasure was denied her. The chill of the room invaded her bones and added to the misery of her hunger, thirst, and hopelessness.

Maranatha got down where she could look Jane Ann in the face.

"He thinks he's going to bring his controllers back with him, capture us, and rescue you. But it won't work because they will never find you."

Now Jane Ann's previous discomfort seemed insignificant compared to the fear that gripped her. This woman was not only paranoid; she was evil.

Jane Ann didn't expect reason to work, but it sounded like she had nothing to lose. "We don't have any controllers or any connection to the government. We were on a trip with my brother and his wife and that guy kidnapped us. He's an escaped convict."

Maranatha looked at Tobiah as if Jane Ann hadn't spoken. "Give me the keys." She walked around the back of the pillory.

Jane Ann breathed in relief. Maybe she was getting through.

Maranatha unlocked the pillory and jerked Jane Ann up by the arm. She efficiently and tightly bound Jane Ann's wrists and then thrust her toward Tobiah.

"Here's your chance to redeem yourself. Take her up to the temple. Another screw-up and you will be banished. Or worse."

Tobiah didn't hesitate. He pulled Jane Ann out the door. There had been moments before when he seemed sympathetic to their plight, but all of that was gone now. She stumbled out into what seemed absolute darkness. But gradually she could make out the shapes of the buildings. Tobiah led her across the open space toward the surrounding hills.

"What...is the temple?" she managed to gasp.

Evidently Tobiah was very eager to make up for his previous transgression with speed and silence. He didn't break stride, even when he reached the rocky hillside, and found a break that led up a rocky path.

Jane Ann couldn't imagine how he knew where he was going in the dark, but he took the path in long strides, tugging her along behind him. She protested a little with no results.

Finally he stopped, reached in a pocket, and pulled out a match. He struck it on the side of his jeans and lit a torch that appeared in the match light. The torch was mounted in a carved out niche that shielded it from being seen directly from outside, but it flared up and threw its light inward to a large cave. From the shadows cast by the light, it was obvious that the cave was not natural—it had been chiseled out by hand.

A large stone, like an altar, stood near the back. Crosses had been carved into the walls. Other than that, it was empty. As Tobiah dragged Jane Ann toward the stone, he lit two other torches along the walls, and it was then that she noticed iron rings embedded in the floor in front of the altar thing. She balked, but he was stronger and pulled her forward.

"No!" she screamed, trying to pummel him with her bound fists. It was no use. He was not only stronger, but he was also determined to get back into Maranatha's good graces. Others entered the cave as Tobiah was trying to get Jane Ann up on the altar, and three of the men ran to help. She struggled and twisted until her arms ached and wrists were sore. Finally, she collapsed, defeated. The men lashed her down with ropes tied to the iron rings.

The crowd parted and Maranatha strode in, minus her gun but brandishing a tall walking stick. She had thrown a light blue robe or sheet or something over her clothes—Jane Ann could see her cowboy boots and pajamas under the robe. The group quieted as she walked up to the altar.

She turned, faced the group, and held up her hands as if for silence, although there was not a sound in the room.

"The time is near. They are sending spies to try and bring us down. This woman is one—a demon disguised as an average person. Azariah is another. He took advantage of my absence last night at supper to blaspheme and make unfounded accusations against our saviors. The Clean are out there. They will land and rescue us when the time is right. We will be taken to a place unsullied by the filth of humanity. We must be patient and keep our ranks free of this scum." She gestured behind her to Jane Ann. "When we have cleansed this place of her, we will bring Azariah up and take care of him as well." There were murmurs and nods throughout the group. Jane Ann turned her face away from them so that they wouldn't see her tears.

FRANNIE WISHED THEY had ridden with the sheriff so they could hear what Mickey was telling them. What was the loony farm? Who shot the tire? Where was Jane Ann locked up? She couldn't make sense of his story, although she guessed being kidnapped twice and shot once might do that to you.

She reached over and put her hand on Larry's arm. "She'll be okay. I know it."

He kept his eyes on the sheriff's taillights. "I wish I believed that."

Frannie didn't know what else to say. She rode in silence until the whomp-whomp of a helicopter became audible over the truck noise. She looked at Larry.

"The State Patrol again?"

"Must be. Don't know who else would be out here."

The sheriff pulled over into the turnaround that they had passed earlier. Larry did likewise, parked, and jumped out of the truck. Frannie followed, and they met between the vehicles with Mickey and the deputy.

"There's a lane hidden behind those rocks," Mickey was saying, as he grabbed the deputy's wrist to point the flashlight she was holding. "It goes back quite a ways.

There's a ranch back there, and these folks are waiting for aliens to rescue them when Armageddon comes. And they think anyone from the outside is a spy sent by the government."

The sheriff nodded. "There's several of those groups around here. Do they have weapons, do you know?"

"Plenty," Mickey said.

"Okay. I've got three more cars coming that should be here any minute. McClarty, you and I will check out this lane, and come back when the rest get here."

"I'm going with you," Mickey said. "She's my wife."

"Me too," Larry said.

"Absolutely not!" Sheriff Parsons said. "I can't be responsible for any extra civilians. You three wait here."

"But I can at least point out which building they were keeping us in," Mickey insisted.

The sheriff slapped his flashlight on his palm a couple of times and looked up at the rocks.

"All right," he said finally. "From your description, you should be able to do that from a distance. It will probably be getting light by the time we get there, and then you two are coming back here."

"I'm not staying here by myself," Frannie said.

"Oh, for Pete's sake!" The sheriff threw up his hands. "McClarty, you stay here with her and come up with the others. By that time your husband should be back. C'mon!" he said in disgust to Larry and Mickey. He pulled his gun and led the way into the dark.

Frannie and Deputy McClarty looked at each other.

"As always, the women are left behind," Frannie said.

McClarty started to protest, and then smiled. "You're right."

"Is Mickey's arm going to be okay?"

"Yeah, it's just a flesh wound. But he needs to have a doctor look at it."

Frannie laughed. "Jane Ann is a retired nurse. She'll have his butt at the nearest ER faster than you can draw that gun." Then she sobered as she thought, *If Jane Ann is okay.*

They could hear cars coming down the road and, in a couple of minutes, three patrol cars pulled off the gravel into the turnaround. A total of eight officers in SWAT gear got out—two women and six men.

McClarty looked at Frannie in hesitation. Frannie waved her hand in a shooing motion. "You go. Someone needs to get them up to speed. Larry and Mickey should be back soon."

"You're sure?"

"Yes, I'll be fine. I'll lock myself in the truck." She spoke with more confidence than she felt, but chided herself that this was not about her. She climbed in the truck and hit the locks. Deputy McClarty led the officers to the hidden lane entrance and, one by one, they disappeared around the corner.

Frannie had lowered the window slightly, and as their voices died away, she was left with the unfamiliar night sounds. Sitting here alone, she could almost believe the alien stories—this landscape and its smells and sounds were so foreign to her. At least she could detect a slight lightening in the east as dawn approached. Hopefully that would make the search for Jane Ann easier, but maybe it would make an actual rescue more difficult. She didn't know.

She leaned her head against the doorpost and realized that it was almost twenty-four hours since she had really slept. So many worries bombarded her — Jane Ann's safety, Mickey's health, Larry and Mickey's safety, what to say to Larry's mother and other siblings. She must have dozed, because she jumped when Larry unlocked the truck door.

"What is it?" she said in alarm.

"No news. But Mickey wants to go back up there. I do too, but I don't want to leave you alone."

"I'll go with you." She opened her door. "You didn't find out anything?"

"Get the binoculars out of the glove compartment," he said. "We may need them."

He helped her along the rocky ground to where Mickey waited by the lane entrance and filled her in on what they had learned. "The sheriff got a report from the chopper. They're using thermal imaging and couldn't find any signs of people in the ranch compound, but there is something up on the hillside."

Frannie wanted to ask more questions, but was out of breath as they climbed the lane. They reached a point where the lane headed back downhill and the dawn light just barely revealed the buildings of the ranch compound. All was quiet, and there was no sign of life. Mickey moved down the lane just far enough that he could point at an area east of where they were standing along the same ridge.

"Somewhere over there, they saw some imaging outlining some of the big boulders. They think there are people hiding in a cave there."

Frannie got a good look at Mickey's face. "Mickey, you're white as a sheet. You'd better sit down." She pointed to a low boulder.

"I need to help find Jane Ann," he said, but let himself be lightly pushed down on the rock.

"Mickey, please, take it from me. We have no weapons, and you are about ready to pass out. We will just be in the way," Larry said.

Voices coming from the area Mickey had pointed out drew their eyes that way. People were emerging from the rocks as if by magic. Mickey got up and started to climb the rocks toward them.

"Mick!" Larry said and pointed. "They're headed down the hill. The cops are in charge." He grabbed Mickey's good arm. "You'll end up on that empty head of yours. We'll go down the lane and meet them."

Mickey hesitated and then let Larry help him back to the lane. "Thanks, buddy," Mickey said, all of his usual sarcasm gone. A strong indication that Mickey was feeling really shaky, Frannie knew.

Between them, Frannie and Larry supported him as they picked their way down the lane to the ranch compound. By that time, the deputies were herding the compound's residents into a long line. The State Patrol helicopter had landed on the open ground between the buildings, and several more officers emerged.

Frannie heard sirens behind them and turned to see several police vans coming through the lane. They were followed by an ambulance.

Mickey strained his neck to search the faces coming down the hillside. "I don't see her." He gripped Frannie's hand and pulled her toward the rocks. Sheriff Parsons appeared, and Larry hurried to meet him. Frannie and Mickey followed as fast as Mickey could go.

"Sheriff!" Larry called out when they got near. "My sister — ?"

Parsons turned, and acknowledged them. "They'll be bringing her down." Frannie tried to read his expression, but his face was stoic. Thinking that did not bode well, her heart sank, and she could see Mickey had the same thoughts. The sheriff rushed off to see to his prisoners.

Mickey started to sink to the ground, and Frannie held on to his arm. "Larry! Help me."

Larry turned from watching the path entrance, saw Mickey's state and hastened to support his brother-in-law as they lowered him to the ground.

"I'm okay..." Mickey said weakly.

"Shut up," Larry said.

Frannie check his forehead. "He's got a fever," she told Larry.

"Jane Ann — " Mickey whispered.

Two EMTs hurried past them toward the path carrying a folded stretcher. "Stay with Mickey," Larry said and followed them up the path, explaining his relationship as they went.

Mickey was leaning against a rock and looked at Frannie with pleading eyes. Frannie sat down beside him and took his hand. "We're going to wait right here. She must be okay, or they would be taking up a body bag, not a stretcher." She hoped that was true. "Tell me what happened here, Mick. Who are these people?" she asked, trying to distract him."

"Some kind of cult—sort of religious and UFO combined." Mickey took a breath. "They're waiting for aliens to rescue them at the Apocalypse or something."

"You mean like Heaven's Gate?"

"Not quite. These guys don't have a date." Mickey almost grinned.

"So who shot your tire out?"

"The leader. Then she brought us here and locked us up in pillories. In that big building over there."

"Pillories? Like—" she pantomimed her head and hands in the stocks.

"You got it."

"Oh my God, how awful!"

Mickey stared toward the path. "What's taking them so long?"

"It's only been a few minutes. Was Badger in the pillory, too?"

"No, they took him to something they called the snake pit. He must have overpowered the young man who took him there."

Frannie shook her head. "This is crazy, Mickey. If we weren't on this trip, and you came home with this story, I wouldn't believe a word you said. Oh! Alice called yesterday and wanted to tell Jane Ann about some high school friend that's visiting. We told her that you probably didn't have phone service. She doesn't know what happened as far as we know. Bob called, too—he heard it on the news and promised not to tell her. But we'll need to contact them all as soon as they bring Jane Ann down."

"If anything happens to her...if she's not okay, I don't know what I'll do, Frannie. This is my fault. I didn't lock the motorhome that night. And last night, Tobiah—the guy who was guarding us—let us take turns sleeping on the floor with our wrists tied to his. I got it untied without waking him, but the keys to the pillory were in his pocket. I wanted to check first to see if they left the keys in the Rocket so we could get away. I knew getting the keys from him would probably wake him, y'see. Then Badger showed up, and the rest you know."

He sank back with the efforts of his speech. Frannie patted him on the arm. "Well, this nightmare is just about over." And she hoped that was true.

It was another twenty minutes before she heard footsteps on the path, with Larry giving directions to the EMTs.

Jane Ann was covered in a heavy blanket and had her face turned away so Frannie could not tell if she was conscious or awake. Mickey didn't care.

"Jane Ann!" He struggled to his feet with Frannie trying to help. Jane Ann turned her head toward them and gave them a weak smile.

Larry stopped the EMTs. "This is her husband and he got grazed by a bullet earlier. You need to take him, too."

"Can he walk?" asked the younger man. "Otherwise we'll come back for him after we get her in the ambulance."

"We'll help him," Larry said.

They made it to the ambulance, and as they loaded the stretcher, Frannie asked them, "Is she going to be all right?"

"She's badly dehydrated and has a lot of bruises. I think she's probably suffering from shock. We'll take her to the local hospital and have them check her out." They helped Mickey into the ambulance.

Before they left, Mickey said to Larry, "Can you get the Rocket?"

"Sure thing."

Mickey tossed him the keys. "Oh, wait—they put somebody else in the snake pit last night—one of their own. It's somewhere behind the main building. Better have the sheriff check it out."

The ambulance took off, lights flashing in the early morning light. Larry and Frannie needed to get back to their truck, but the police vans were starting back up the lane. They walked over to Sheriff Parsons who stood shaking his head. "We got way too many of these goonies, and I don't care as long as they keep to themselves. But this mess..."

Larry said, "Sheriff, Mickey says last night they put someone in what they call the snake pit. He said it's behind the biggest building."

Parson raised his eyebrows and beckoned another deputy over to him. As they headed to check out the story, Larry called after him "We'll be at the hospital!"

They sheriff waved them off, and they started up the lane.

CHAPTER TWENTY ONE
FRIDAY

OWING TO THE EARLY hour, the parking lot of the hospital was fairly empty. Larry parked the Rocket in two spaces at the back of the lot, and Frannie pulled their truck in next to it. They locked up both vehicles and hurried to the emergency entrance. Larry showed his ID to the receptionist and explained his relationship to Mickey and Jane Ann. She guided them back to two cubicles, the curtain open between them, where Mickey was vocally protesting something from one bed, while Jane Ann lay quietly in the other, hooked up to numerous monitors and tubes.

She glanced at them, smiled a little, and whispered, "Hi."

Mickey looked up from fussing with his IV and said "Get us out of here."

"Nice to see that you're being a good patient, Ferraro." Larry grinned and clutched his sister's hand. "Hey, Sis. First thing, we have to come up with a story to tell Mom."

"It hasn't been on the news?" Jane Ann said. Her voice was raw.

"Yeah, but to my knowledge, she hasn't seen it."

"We'll have to tell her. Otherwise, someone else will, and then we'll be in even more trouble."

"Well, not like it would be the first time. Remember when we painted the basement floor for that play you wanted to put on? It was your idea, but I got blamed."

She grinned. "Really, a path and a pond improved that basement tremendously."

"What does the doctor say?" Frannie asked.

"They might release us later today. We're both dehydrated and need rest. We haven't slept much since yesterday morning."

"I'm fine now," Mickey said. "I'm ready to go." He tried to sit up.

Jane Ann looked stricken. "Mick, don't leave me here alone!"

Mickey's demeanor changed immediately, and he sank back in his bed. "Oh, no way, honey. I didn't mean that."

Larry looked at them both. "Here's the plan. You guys stay here and do exactly as you're told to do. We'll leave you Frannie's phone. We picked up the Rocket, and we'll take it back to the campground and hook it up. I'll talk to Mom, and try to at least downplay the story. When they give you the okay, we'll come back and get you."

"Sounds good," Jane Ann said. She looked like she was about to nod off. Frannie and Larry gave them awkward hugs and left. Larry gave his phone number to the receptionist and asked to be notified of any change.

171

Frannie followed Larry with the pickup, so there was no chance for conversation until they returned to the campground. Larry made the necessary hookups to the Rocket, and Frannie went inside to straighten things and wipe down the counters. She picked up candy bar wrappers off the floor that she knew neither Mickey nor Jane Ann would have thrown there. She wondered if, having spent so much time in their beloved coach with someone like Badger and in fear for their lives, they would ever be really comfortable in it again. She opened a couple of windows to let the brisk outside air take away the stuffiness and the bad vibes.

When she came out, Larry had disappeared into their trailer. Once inside, she saw the table laid with plates of leftover Chinese takeout and steaming mugs of coffee.

Larry gave a sweeping gesture with his hand. "Lunch, m'dear?"

"How lovely," Frannie said. "When did we last eat?" She slid into the dinette bench.

"Back in aught-eight, I think."

She took a big bite of her sandwich. "Ummm. Food for the Gods. Don't forget, you need to call your mom as soon as we're done."

Larry grimaced. "How about we wait until Easter?" Then he noticed her look. "I know. I know. I'll call her. But I'm not going to give her the whole story."

"We don't even know the whole story yet."

A knock at the door startled them, and Larry got up to answer it.

Sheriff Parsons stood on the steps peering up at him.

"Come in, Sheriff. Have a seat."

He did, rubbing his eyes. "Been a long night...for all of us."

"How about some coffee?"

"That sounds great." He sat forward in his chair. "Well, Badger is on his way again to Los Cruces — this time in a patrol car with two deputies. He'll be coming back later to stand trial for murder, assault, and abduction."

Frannie scraped up bits of vegetables with her fork and took her plate to the sink. "What about those cult people?"

"Maranatha — we're still trying to find her real name — has been charged with attempted murder, and various others with conspiracy to commit murder. We're still trying to sort all of that out."

Frannie turned to face him. "Were they going to kill Jane Ann? Why?"

"It looks like it. We don't know why — none of them are talking, but they were paranoid about anyone from the outside. It seems that maybe they thought she was responsible somehow for Badger's and Mr. Ferraro's escape, although that makes no sense. But sense doesn't have much to do with any of this. I haven't been to the hospital yet. How are your sister and brother-in-law doing?"

Larry said, "They thought they'd be released later today."

"Good. Do you know how long you plan to stay here?"

"I'm guessing we will be outta here as soon as they feel up to it. As beautiful as it is here, I think we'll all be ready for some new scenery." Larry gave a wry smile that didn't extend to his eyes.

The sheriff stood and took his mug to the sink. "I don't blame you. I think I'll go to the hospital to see if they're up to giving statements."

"Sheriff, will we all be required to come back for the trials?" Frannie asked.

He shrugged. "I don't know. They might be satisfied with depositions, which you could give at your local courthouse. Well, I'll talk to you folks later." He touched his hat and was gone.

"Just like the Lone Ranger," Larry said, picked up his phone as it rang, and glanced at the screen. "Bob."

He updated his brother on Jane Ann's rescue and condition. "I know — I was just going to call her when you called. We'll give her a softened version of the story...yeah, thanks...I'll tell her and have her call you when she gets rested up."

As he clicked off the phone, he said, "I guess I can't put it off any longer." He dialed his mother. Frannie cleared the dishes while he talked, and even though he tried to downplay the danger, it was clear from his side of the conversation that Alice Shoemaker was very alarmed. Larry assured her that Jane Ann and Mickey were fine now, that he would have Jane Ann call, and that they would be headed home when they left here, probably the next day.

"Whew!" he sighed, when he finished. "But if it was Sam or Sally, we would feel pretty helpless and scared, too."

Frannie went to him and hugged him. They stood in a clench for a few minutes, each trying to push back their fears and thoughts.

"Well," Larry said, as he wiped his eyes and gently pushed her back, "I think I'll get the atlas and work out a route home. I doubt if we want to continue on to Santa Fe."

"Good idea," Frannie said. She finished putting away the dishes and sandwich makings, while he went to get the atlas out of the truck.

Together they pored over the maps, selecting the quickest route home with reasonable drives each day. Frannie threw some frozen meatballs, veggies, and canned tomatoes in the crockpot and was just jotting down their proposed stops in a notebook when Larry's phone rang. It was Mickey and Larry put it on speaker.

"Jane Ann badgered the doctors into releasing us—" they could hear Jane Ann in the background ordering *'Don't say badger!'* —"and the sheriff is going to bring us back."

"Okay, great."

"See you then."

They went outside to wait.

"It's too bad," Frannie said, as she looked around. "It's beautiful country, but it will never look the same again to me."

"It's not really New Mexico's fault."

"Oh, I know. It just feels different--scary."

Palmer and Peg Pierce walked down the road toward them, waving.

"You're still here!" Frannie said when they got close.

"We heard this morning that your family was rescued. We just couldn't leave without finding out if everyone was all right, and how you are doing," Peg said.

Palmer shrugged. "We're not in any hurry anyway. So what's the situation?"

"That's very nice of you. Come in—we expect them back any time," Frannie said. "We are so relieved, as you can imagine." She led the way into their camper.

"This is so cozy," Peg said as she looked around at Frannie's 'cabin-y touches: denim slipcovers and checked curtains.

"Thank you," Frannie said. "Have a seat. Can I get you anything?"

"No, no," Palmer said. "We won't stay. But what happened? How did you find them?"

Frannie smiled at Palmer's implication that they had done it one their own. Larry filled them in on the call from the sheriff in the middle of the night and the events that had transpired since then.

"Wow!" Palmer said, and shook his head. "That is amazing."

Peg sat forward. "They were held prisoner in pillories?"

"That's what they said," Frannie said. "I could see marks on Jane Ann's neck."

They heard a car pull up. "We'll go," Palmer said. "I'm sure you all need some rest."

"Bed will feel good tonight," Frannie agreed. "And I hope this is as close as you get to any excitement on the rest of your trip."

Palmer handed her a business card. "My email is on there; please let us know that you get home okay."

They all went outside as Mickey was helping Jane Ann out of the sheriff's cruiser. Frannie gave Peg and Palmer each a hug, and she and Larry thanked the couple for their concern. Frannie went to Jane Ann's other side.

"I'm really okay," she insisted, and tried to shake them off.

"Just give yourself a little more time," Frannie said. "I don't want you keeling over on us and leaving me alone here with these two."

"You're right...but that's the only reason I'm agreeing."

But as they neared the Rocket, Jane Ann balked a little.

"Do you want to come in our camper? We can get your clothes and you can use our shower and even sleep there if you want."

Jane Ann considered but shook her head. "No, I need to do this."

Once she was inside, she looked around and smiled at Frannie. "You cleaned it up."

"Just a little. I have some soup in the crockpot. I'm guessing you might want to clean up and change clothes?"

"Oh, yes. And soup sounds great. Here or at your place?"

"Where would you prefer?"

"Let's do it over there. Easier for you and I can get reacquainted with the Rocket slowly." She looked at her watch. "Do I have time for a short nap, too?"

"All the time you need. And we've mapped out a possible route home—we can talk about that over supper." Frannie gave Jane Ann another hug and dissolved into tears.

"Hey!" Mickey said. "I was kidnapped, too—twice in fact." So Frannie hugged him and then wiped her eyes and turned back to Jane Ann. "Do you need any help, or should we skedaddle?"

"Skedaddle. Did you talk to Mom?" she asked Larry.

"I did, and I'm afraid you're going to have to call her as soon as you feel up to it."

Jane Ann sighed. "I'd better do that first."

AN HOUR LATER, they had settled around the little dinette with bowls of steaming soup that Frannie had concocted out of findings in the cupboard and refrigerator.

"It's amazing," she said, as she put some warmed-up breadsticks on the table, "we just went to the store a couple of days ago and have hardly eaten here since, but I don't seem to have much to make a full meal."

"You did great. This looks wonderful," Jane Ann said.

Mickey took a big bite of soup. "Of course, you realize, Frannie, that warmed over cardboard would look good—ouch!" He rubbed his good arm where his wife had pinched him.

"How can you say something like that?"

Frannie laughed. "Actually, it's a relief. Now we know for sure that the cult didn't replace him with some alien being. So tell us the story. Begin with the abduction."

And they did. Through the meal, with seconds for Jane Ann and Mickey, during a hastily constructed desert of pound cake and strawberries out of the freezer, and over glasses of wine settled around the living room. Larry and Frannie filled in events from their side of things. By the time they had finished, Jane Ann looked pretty peaked, and even Mickey had wound down.

Larry was shaking his head. "Wow. I think this beats all of our previous episodes." He looked at his wife. "Not to belittle the time you were kidnapped, Frannie," he hastened to add.

"I agree," Frannie said. "That was only a few hours, and at least we were in our own territory. And not held by a group of crazies."

"They aren't all crazy. Just one of those scary situations where a lot of unhappy or disenfranchised

179

people got sucked in by one person's crazy visions." Mickey finished and looked around at their astonished faces. "What?"

"You scare us when you get serious and make sense," Larry said.

Jane Ann got up. "I'll take him home and put him to bed. He'll be himself in the morning."

HAPPY CAMPER TIPS

Happy Camper Tip #1

This tasty stew can be done on the stove or in a cast iron Dutch oven over a fire.

Chorizo, Sweet Potato and Brown Rice Stew: Brown three chorizo sausages--about one pound. Add one large onion, chopped, one clove garlic, crushed, and 1/2 tsp paprika. Cook for 4-5 minutes or until onion is tender. Add two (14 oz cans) diced tomatoes, 1 (14 oz) can chickpeas, drained and rinsed, and 1 or 2 large sweet potatoes, peeled, chopped. Add 1 cup of water and 3/4-1 cup brown rice. Bring to a boil, reduce heat to low, then simmer for 10-15 minutes or until sweet potato is just tender and rice is cooked. Stir through 1/4 cup of chopped parsley and season to taste.

Happy Camper Tip #2

Hanging storage with pockets, such as shoe bags, have a multitude of uses. They can be hung over doors and used for, besides shoes, cords, tools, grooming items, kitchen utensils, etc. Some people cut them in two or three strips and tack them to the top edge of under-the-bed storage, to provide space for shoes and other items along the side of the bed under the overhanging mattress. Ones with smaller pockets can be used inside cabinet doors.

Happy Camper Tip #3

Foil Packet Dinners: Many of us grew up with 'hobo' dinners: some hamburger, potatoes and carrots, wrapped in foil and cooked over the fire at Scout or church camp. The same principle can be combined to almost any entrees. A favorite of ours is salmon filets with fresh asparagus. Spray a large square of foil with non-stick cooking spray first and arrange 6-10 stalks of asparagus in a row. Lay a large salmon filet or two small ones on the asparagus. Mix a tablespoon of butter, some chopped garlic, and a tablespoon of shredded Parmesan cheese, and spread it on the filets. Sprinkle with salt and pepper and top with two or three slices of lemon. Variations in the topping can include Dijon mustard, chopped red pepper or tomato. Bring the sides of the foil up and seal; fold over the ends and do the same. Make more packets for each person you are serving.

Lay on the grill and cook over hot coals for 30-40 minutes. No need to turn over. Check occasionally; when the asparagus is fork tender, the filets should be done. Add a nice fruit salad and maybe some bread or rolls from a nearby local bakery for a perfect light supper for a summer evening. No pans to wash!

Happy Camper Tip #4

Alien Faces Cookies: What could be a more perfect recipe for The Space Invader?

Cream 1/2 cup butter, 1/4 cup shortening and 1 cup granulated sugar with electric mixer on medium speed for 1 to 2 minutes. Mix in 2 tablespoons light corn syrup, 2 large eggs, 1 teaspoon vanilla, 1/2 teaspoon almond extract and 1/8 teaspoonsalt; mix until fluffy. Sift together 1-3/4 cups flour and 1 teaspoon baking powder and stir into sugar mixture; blend well. Cover dough; refrigerate 2 to 3 hours.

Preheat oven to 375°F. Sprinkle flat surface with flour and roll out dough to 1/4-inch thickness. Cut out faces with oval or egg shaped cookie cutters. Use edge of a teaspoon to form teardrop-shaped eyes. Place cookies on ungreased cookie sheet. Bake 8 to 10 minutes or until sides begin to brown slightly. Cool on cooling rack positioned over sheet of waxed paper.

To make glaze, sift 2 1/2 cups confectioners' sugar and add up to 1/3 cup of cream, tablespoon by tablespoon, until smooth and thin. Pour glaze over cooled cookies on rack. (Waxed paper will catch drips.) Once glaze is dry, decorate faces with black gel or use sliced black gumdrops to make eyes. —Suzanne Collier

Happy Camper Tip #5

Sliders:

1 large onion, finely minced

Kosher salt

1 1/8 pounds freshly ground beef

1 medium onion, peeled and grated on the medium holes of a box grater, juices and pulp reserved (about 1 1/2 cups)

Freshly ground black pepper

12 slices American cheese (optional)

16 slider-sized buns (about 2 1/2- to 3-inches across)

24 thin dill pickle slices

Condiments, as desired

Toss diced onion with 1 teaspoon Kosher salt in medium bowl. Set aside at room temperature until fragrant, about 10 minutes. Meanwhile, divide ground beef into 12 evenly sized balls. Using damp hands, press balls into even, patties approximately 1/8th-inch thick, and 3 1/2-inches wide. Place on large plastic-wrap lined plate. Patties can be stacked with layer of plastic wrap between each layer. Place in refrigerator until ready to cook.

Preheat heavy-bottomed 12-inch skillet over medium low heat until evenly heated, about 5 minutes. Reduce heat to low, and add half of diced onion, using spatula to spread into even layer across bottom of pan. Cook without moving until bottom of onions starts turning pale golden brown, about five minutes (onions should barely sizzle while cooking--adjust heat as necessary).

Add half of grated onions and their juice to skillet. Stir onions with rubber spatula to release browned bits from bottom of pan and spread into thin, even layer. Arrange six hamburger patties on top of onion mixture. Season top of patties with salt and pepper. Add 6 slices of American cheese if desired. Place bun bottoms, cut-side-down, on top of patties. Place bun tops, cut-side-down, on top of bun bottoms, staggering arrangement to maximize exposure to steam.

Continue cooking over low heat until burgers are cooked through and cheese is fully melted, about 3 minutes, adding extra onion juice if pan runs dry, making sure to reserve at least half for second batch (there should be no sizzling sound, and mixture should steam constantly--in some rare cases, substituting water may be necessary if onion juice all runs out). Remove from heat.

Lift burger and bun with spatula. Pick up bun top, invert, and place underneath spatula (burger should now be fully assembled, upside down). Slide spatula out from between burger and bun top. Invert, and place on plate. Repeat with remaining 5 burgers. Spoon any remaining onions and melted cheese in skillet on top of each burger patty, along with two pickles, and condiments as desired. Consume immediately, before repeating with remaining 6 sliders. — Jan Long

Happy Camper Tip #6

Ken's Camping Ten Commandments

I. After set up, never move your tow vehicle without disconnecting your RV.

II. If you have raised the jacks on your trailer or 5th wheel such that your tow vehicle's rear wheels are off the ground, lower the jacks and disconnect your tow vehicle.

III. Never test the power pedestal at the campsite with your tongue.

IV. Avoid opening the valves on your black and gray tanks before connecting the sewer hose.

V. I do not recommend Flambe' cooking inside the RV.

VI. Never sell your old RV to a friend.

VII. Avoid opening your slide into a tree.

VIII. Don't forget your air conditioner when driving into a self-service car wash.

IX. Ensure your TV antenna is down when you leave the campground. It makes one look like a real amateur.

X. Avoid traveling with your awning deployed. — Ken Hald

Happy Camper Tip #7

Avoiding the Pests: Put Bounce dryer sheets in drawers, linen, cabinets when your RV is not used. We never have critters invade, period! — Becky Abraham

Happy Camper Tip #8

Easy Supper: Thaw frozen raw, peeled, shrimp. Marinade an hour or so in Zesty Italian dressing, minced garlic, and a splash of Chardonnay. (the rest of the Chardonnay to be consumed by the cook and friends). Put the shrimp in an aluminum pan on the grill and cook just until white. Add a salad, potato (I microwave ours), and there you have it!! Let's go somewhere! —Becky Abraham

Happy Camper Tip #9

My camping tip is to always take a pocket mirror on the trip! In case you get lost or need help, it is a great way to signal that you need help. You can reflect the sunlight into the sky to get attention and even use morse code to communicate with helicopters and airplanes. —Rich Kent

Happy Camper Tip #10

Flag It! Need a paper towel occasionally when you're cooking outdoors? Use an iron garden flag stand as a paper towel holder. —Star Kent

Happy Camper Tip #11

Grilled Cabbage Steaks (Serves: 6)

6 slices bacon

1 package McCormick® Grill Mates® Smoky Applewood Marinade

3 tablespoons vegetable oil

2 tablespoons cider vinegar

2 tablespoons maple syrup

1 head green cabbage, cut into 3/4-inch thick slices (about 6 steaks)

1/2 cup crumbled blue cheese

2 tablespoons thinly sliced green onions

Cook bacon in large skillet on medium heat until crisp. Reserve 1 tablespoon of the drippings. Crumble bacon; set aside. Mix Marinade Mix, oil, vinegar, maple syrup and reserved bacon drippings in small bowl until well blended. Place cabbage steaks in large resealable plastic bag or glass dish. Add marinade; turn to coat well. Refrigerate 30 minutes or longer for extra flavor. Remove cabbage steaks from marinade. Reserve any leftover marinade. Grill cabbage steaks over medium heat 5 to 6 minutes per side or until tender-crisp, brushing with leftover marinade. Serve cabbage steaks topped with blue cheese, crumbled bacon and green onions.

Happy Camper Tip #12

Use the Fresh Water Hose to Save Your RV Slide Out: Worried about the slideout hitting an object like the power pedestal or a tree when setting up at the campsite? Some of us aren't that good at estimating distances.

Add some tape on your fresh water hose marking the width of the slide out when it's fully extended. Now you have a convenient way to measure the available space before opening the slide out. www.loveyourrv.com

Happy Camper Tip #13

A Stitch in Time: Although mending isn't as common an occupation as it used to be, sometimes a lost button or ripped seam in you favorite camping shirt makes it a necessary task. Space is always an issue and I found that three sewing machine bobbins filled with black, white and brown thread, a small packet of needles, and a couple of white and black buttons would fit in a very small box and make an adequate emergency sewing kit.

Happy Camper Tip #14

Zucchini Spice Cake: A great take-along on a camping trip in the summer, when you are inundated with zucchini.

Combine 1/2 cup vegetable oil, 1/3 cup milk, and 2 eggs. Mix 1 1/4 cup granulated sugar, 1 teaspoon baking soda, 2 cups flour (I use 1 cup whole wheat flour and 1 cup all-purpose flour, 1 teaspoon salt, 1/4 teaspoon ground allspice, 1 teaspoon cinnamon, 1/4 teaspoon ground cloves and add to egg mixture. Stir in 2 cups grated unpeeled zucchini. Pour in greased and floured 9 x 13 pan.

Sprinkle with Crunchy Topping: Stir together 1/3 cup flour, 1/2 teaspoon cinnamon, 1/4 cup nuts, 1/4 cup brown sugar and cut in 2 tablespoons butter. Bake in 350 oven 40 minutes or until the cake tests done.

Note: I tried this once substituting unsweetened applesauce for the oil. Not a good decision.

Happy Camper Tip #15

Outdoor Living: The idea of camping is to spend time outdoors (No, really!), enjoying the beauties of nature. Sometimes, of course, nature doesn't cooperate, but when it does, cooking, eating, playing games, and reading a new Frannie Shoemaker mystery are better outdoors than in.

Many campsites have nice gravel or cement pads, but grassy areas can be great too. After all, it is nature. For us, comfortable chairs are a requirement and bag chairs don't meet that comfortable part. We like the camp chairs with fold up trays and a solid bar on the bottom connecting the pairs of legs. Those bars prevent the chair from sinking into the soft ground. We also like the antigravity reclining lawn chairs. Small folding tables are also very handy for chairs without fold up trays.

Most sites have picnic tables, and condition may range from new and/or pristine to possibly ready for a dumpster. Vinyl tablecloths can cover the table and make a clean if not level surface. A word about busy patterns: if you play a lot of games, those pattern can make it hard to distinguish playing pieces, cards, or dominos. The wind can play havoc with tablecloths, and I've found that the plastic or metal clips sold for the purpose of holding the cloth on the table generally aren't designed for the thickness of the tables in parks. There are also spring loaded weights that attach to the edge of the cloth and work well most of the time.

Small folding tables, usually metal or plastic, are handy beside the chairs or near the firepit when cooking. Some kind of rug for use at least by the camper entrance to catch some of the debris, and many people use larger outdoor rugs or artificial turf to cover their sitting area.

Lights are another important addition; strings can be attached to awnings with clips. The advent of LED and solar lights are a tremendous boon to the camper. We carry a set of solar stake garden lights and use them to outline our campsite, or highlight stumps that might cause a spill in the dark.

All of this paraphernalia takes space, as well as time to pack and unpack it. Decide how you want to use your outdoor space and then what you need most to carry on those activities.

Happy Camper Tip #16

S'more Treats:

6 ounces (about 1 cup) miniature chocolate chips

6 cups graham cereal, like Golden Grahams

1 package (10 ounces, or about 6 cups) miniature marshmallows

5 tablespoons (2.5 oz) butter

1/4 tsp salt

1 tsp vanilla extract

Place the miniature chocolate chips in the freezer to chill while you prepare the rest of the recipe. Line a 9x13 pan with aluminum foil and spray the foil with nonstick cooking spray. Spray a large bowl with nonstick cooking spray, and pour the graham cereal into the bowl. Add 1 cup of miniature marshmallows to the cereal. In a large microwave-safe bowl, combine the butter and the remaining package of miniature marshmallows.

Microwave them together for 1 minute, then stir. If the marshmallows are not fully melted, continue to microwave in short 20-second bursts, stirring after every interval, until the marshmallows and butter are completely smooth. Add the salt and vanilla extract and stir them in.

Pour the marshmallow mixture over the cereal mixture in the large bowl, and stir until the cereal is coated. Finally, add the frozen chocolate chips and stir them in briefly, trying not to stir too much to avoid melting the chips. Scrape the candy into the prepared 9x13 pan and press it into an even layer. Let it set at room temperature, for about an hour. To serve, remove the candy from the pan using the foil as handles and cut it into small squares.

Store S'mores Treats in an airtight container at room temperature. This candy is best enjoyed within a few days of making it, since the cereal will start to get soft and stale after a few days.

Happy Camper Tip #17

Grilled Pineapple Chicken Foil Packets: - chicken, pineapple, peppers, and onions slathered in a sweet and savory teriyaki sauce and cooked on the grill!

Preheat the grill. Lay out 4 large (about 24 inches long) pieces of foil. In a bowl whisk together 1 cup teriyaki sauce and 1 cup Asian toasted sesame dressing. Cut 4 boneless skinless chicken breasts into 1 1/2 inch pieces. Chop one green pepper, 1 red pepper, and 1 small onion. Distribute chicken, peppers, onions, 1 can of pineapple chunks, and sauce between the sheets of foil. Fold the sides of the foil over the fillings and seal shut.

Grill packets for about 10-15 minutes, turning over once half way through. Carefully unfold foil packets and check chicken to make sure it is cooked through. Garnish with cilantro and sesame seeds if desired, serve immediately.

Happy Camper Tip #18

The Long and the Short of It: Most of the summer we take short three or four day trips, and our planning and packing is quite different than the longer trips we have taken in the spring and the fall.

For a few days, we often take along salads and other side dishes prepared at home and cook our entree at the campsite, usually over an open fire. A couple of towels and changes of clothes will suffice. We don't worry about laundry soap or quarters for the laundromat. Our pantry does not include much in the way of staples, such as pasta, rice, baking supplies, or canned goods unless they are planned for a specific dish that trip.

But when we take trips of several weeks, that all changes. More towels and laundry supplies are included. Pasta, rice, and even a few convenience side dish packets that can be combined with frozen meatballs or grilled chicken strips are stocked. How do we find room for this? A careful check of what is filling the cabinets and cubbies usually reveals a few things that don't need to go. For example, I had six cafeteria trays that the grandchildren enjoyed when they were along. But they don't go on these trips, and the trays not only take up a lot of space, they are heavy. So out they go. And there are other things that if it's just the two of us, or maybe one other couple, we don't need.

Happy Camper Tip #19

Wild Rice, Butter Bean, and Garlic Roasted Carrot Salad: Preheat the oven to 400F. Wash 4-5 medium carrots and slice them on the diagonal into 'coins', or peel 1 or 2 sweet potatoes and cut them into chunks. Place on a baking sheet. Mince 4 cloves of garlic and combine it with 2 tablespoons of olive oil. Pour over carrots   or potaoes and toss to coat. Sprinkle with sea salt. Place in the oven and roast, turning them a few times over the course of 15-20 minutes.

Cook rice according to directions.

Make the dressing by combining 1 Tbsp. mustard, 1 Tbsp. maple syrup, 2 Tbsp. apple cider vinegar, 3 Tbsp. extra virgin olive oil and a pinch of sea salt and shake well.

Pour dressing over warm rice and toss. Let sit for 5 minutes or so. Mix with beans. Toss in the carrots, scraping the pan to add garlic oil to the remainder of the ingredients. Throw in some paper-thin red onion slices, a heap of fresh, chopped dill, and grind some black pepper to finish.

Happy Camper Tip #20

Creamy Italian Sausage Tortellini Soup: On cool nights of camping, nothing quite hits the spot like soup. This one is different from the run-of-the-mill soups and really warms you up!

In a large Dutch oven or pot, heat 2 tablespoons olive oil over medium-high heat and sauté 1 yellow onion, chopped, for 6-8 minutes, or until softened and translucent. Season with Kosher salt and freshly ground pepper.

Add 1 pound mild Italian sausage to pot and cook, stirring frequently, until brown and crumbled into bite-sized pieces. Stir in 3 cloves minced garlic and cook for 1 minute, or until fragrant.

Mix in 1 can diced tomatoes and 12 ounces fresh or frozen tortellini, then pour in 1 cup low sodium chicken broth and 2/3 cup heavy cream. Season with 1 teaspoon each dried basil and oregano, then season with salt and pepper.

Bring mixture to a boil, then reduce heat to low and let simmer, covered, for 15 minutes, or until pasta is al dente.

Add 2 cups fresh spinach and cook for another 2 minutes, or until just wilted, then remove from heat and serve hot. Garnish with fresh basil. — Harriet Hald

Happy Camper Tip #21

Bottomless Lakes State Park is a state park in New Mexico, located along the Pecos River, about 15 miles southeast of Roswell. It takes its name from nine small, deep lakes located along the eastern escarpment of the Pecos River valley. The escarpment is an ancient limestone reef. Caves formed within the limestone, and as the Pecos River eroded the escarpment, the caves eventually collapsed, leaving behind several deep, almost circular lakes known as cenotes.

ACKNOWLEDGMENTS

The roots of this story were in an incident when we were traveling through New Mexico. Two convicts escaped near Roswell while being transported. We were stopped by a road block for a search, but because our camper had been locked all day, they didn't think it was necessary to search it. We were not abducted by the escapees. The park is very loosely based on Bottomless Lake State Park.

Thank you also to my readers who submitted camping hints and recipes. And to my great beta readers, Elaine, Marcia, and Ginge.

ABOUT THE AUTHOR

Karen Musser Nortman is the author of the Frannie Shoemaker Campground cozy mystery series, including the BRAGMedallion honoree, *Bats and Bones*. After previous incarnations as a secondary social studies teacher (22 years) and a test developer (18 years), she returned to her childhood dream of writing a novel. The Frannie Shoemaker Campground Mysteries came out of numerous 'round the campfire' discussions, making up answers to questions raised by the peephole glimpses one gets into the lives of fellow campers. Where did those people disappear to for the last two days? What kinds of bones are in this fire pit? Why is that woman wearing heels to the shower house?

Karen and her husband Butch originally tent camped when their children were young and switched to a travel trailer when sleeping on the ground lost its romantic adventure. They take frequent weekend jaunts with friends to parks in Iowa and surrounding states, plus occasional longer trips. Entertainment on these trips has ranged from geocaching and hiking/biking to barbecue contests, balloon fests, and buck skinners' rendezvous.

Sign up for Karen's email list at www.karenmussernortman.com and receive a free ereader download of The Blue Coyote..

OTHER BOOKS BY THE AUTHOR

THE AWARD-WINNING FRANNIE SHOEMAKER CAMPGROUND MYSTERIES:

Bats and Bones: (An IndieBRAG Medallion honoree) Frannie and Larry Shoemaker are retirees who enjoy weekend camping with their friends in state parks. They anticipate the usual hiking, campfires, good food, and interesting side trips among the bluffs of beautiful Bat Cave State Park for the long Fourth of July weekend — until a dead body turns up. Confined in the campground and surrounded by strangers, Frannie is drawn into the investigation. Frannie's persistence and curiosity helps authorities sort through the possible suspects and motives, but almost ends her new sleuth career — and her life — for good.

The Blue Coyote: (An IndieBRAG Medallion honoree and a 2013 Chanticleer CLUE finalist) Frannie and Larry Shoemaker love taking their grandchildren, Sabet and Joe, camping with them. But at Bluffs State Park, Frannie finds herself worrying more than usual about their safety, and when another young girl disappears from the campground in broad daylight, her fears increase. The fun of a bike ride, a flea market, marshmallow guns, and a storyteller are quickly overshadowed. Accusations against Larry and her add to the cloud over their heads.

Peete and Repeat: (An IndieBRAG Medallion honoree, 2013 Chanticleer CLUE finalist, and 2014 Chanticleer Mystery and Mayhem finalist) A biking and camping trip to southeastern Minnesota turns into double trouble for Frannie Shoemaker and her friends as she deals with a canoeing mishap and a couple of bodies. Strange happenings in the campground, the nearby nature learning center, and an old power plant complicate the suspect pool and Frannie tries to stay out of it--really--but what can she do?

The Lady of the Lake: (An IndieBRAG Medallion honoree, 2014 Chanticleer CLUE finalist) A trip down memory lane is fine if you don't stumble on a body. Frannie Shoemaker and her friends camp at Old Dam Trail State Park near one of Donna Nowak's childhood homes. They take in the county fair, reminisce at a Fifties-Sixties dance, and check out old hangouts. But the present intrudes when a body surfaces. Donna becomes the focus of the investigation and Frannie wonders if the police shouldn't be looking closer at the victim's many enemies. A traveling goddess worshipper, a mystery writer and the Sisters on the Fly add color to the campground.

To Cache a Killer: Geocaching isn't supposed to be about finding dead bodies. But when retiree, Frannie Shoemaker go camping, standard definitions don't apply. A weekend in a beautiful state park in Iowa buzzes with fund-raising events, a search for Ninja turtles, a bevy of suspects, and lots of great food. But are the campers in the wrong place at the wrong time once too often?

A Campy Christmas: A Holiday novella. The Shoemakers and Ferraros plan to spend Christmas in Texas and then take a camping trip through the Southwest. But those plans are stopped cold when they hit a rogue ice storm in Missouri and they end up snowbound in a campground. And that's just the beginning. Includes recipes and winter camping tips.

Happy Camper Tips and Recipes: All of the tips and recipes from the first four Frannie Shoemaker books in one convenient paperback or Kindle version that you can keep in your camping supplies.

THE TIME TRAVEL TRAILER SERIES

The Time Travel Trailer: (An IndieBRAG Medallion honoree, 2015 Chanticleer Paranormal First-in-Category winner) A 1937 vintage camper trailer half hidden in weeds catches Lynne McBriar's eye when she is visiting an elderly friend Ben. Ben eagerly sells it to her and she just as eagerly embarks on a restoration. But after each remodel, sleeping in the trailer lands Lynne and her daughter Dinah in a previous decade—exciting, yet frightening. Glimpses of their home town and ancestors fifty or sixty years earlier is exciting and also offers some clues to the mystery of Ben's lost love. But when Dinah makes a trip on her own, separating herself from her mother by decades, Lynne has never known such fear. It is a trip that may upset the future if Lynne and her estranged husband can't team up to bring their daughter back.

Trailer on the Fly: How many of us have wished at some time or other we could go back in time and change an action or a decision or just take back something that was said? But it is what it is. There is no rewind, reboot, delete key or any other trick to change the past, right?

Lynne McBriar can. She bought a 1937 camper that turned out to be a time portal. And when she meets a young woman who suffers from serious depression over the loss of a close friend ten years earlier, she has the power to do something about it. And there is no reason not to use that power. Right?

66384426R00129

Made in the USA
Charleston, SC
17 January 2017